W9-BWE-302

j Coh
Cohen, Tish, 1963-

The one and only Zoe Lama

WITHDRAWN

The One and Only Zoë Lama

ALSO BY TISH COHEN
The Invisible Rules of the Zoë Lama

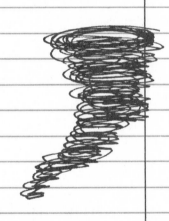

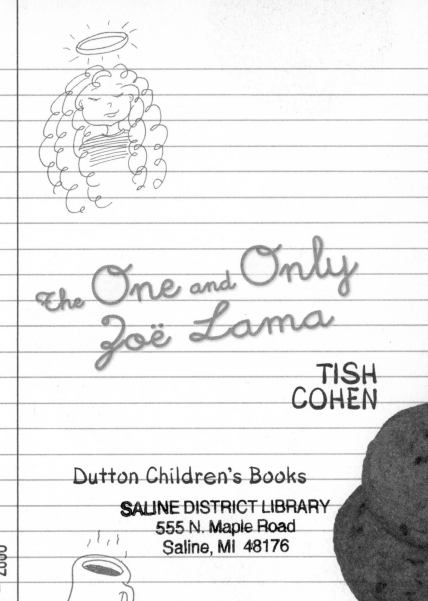

The One and Only Zoë Lama

TISH COHEN

Dutton Children's Books

SALINE DISTRICT LIBRARY
555 N. Maple Road
Saline, MI 48176

AUG - - 2008

DUTTON CHILDREN'S BOOKS
A division of Penguin Young Readers Group
Published by the Penguin Group
Penguin Group (USA) Inc., 375 Hudson Street, New York, New York 10014, U.S.A. • Penguin Group
(Canada), 90 Eglinton Avenue East, Suite 700, Toronto, Ontario, Canada M4P 2Y3 (a division of Pear-
son Penguin Canada Inc.) • Penguin Books Ltd, 80 Strand, London WC2R 0RL, England • Penguin
Ireland, 25 St Stephen's Green, Dublin 2, Ireland (a division of Penguin Books Ltd) • Penguin Group
(Australia), 250 Camberwell Road, Camberwell, Victoria 3124, Australia (a division of Pearson Australia
Group Pty Ltd) • Penguin Books India Pvt Ltd, 11 Community Centre, Panchsheel Park, New Delhi
- 110 017, India • Penguin Group (NZ), 67 Apollo Drive, Rosedale, North Shore 0632, New Zealand
(a division of Pearson New Zealand Ltd) • Penguin Books (South Africa) (Pty) Ltd, 24 Sturdee Avenue,
Rosebank, Johannesburg 2196, South Africa
Penguin Books Ltd, Registered Offices: 80 Strand, London WC2R 0RL, England

This book is a work of fiction. Names, characters, places, and incidents are either the product of the
author's imagination or are used fictitiously, and any resemblance to actual persons, living or dead,
business establishments, events, or locales is entirely coincidental.

Copyright © 2008 by Tish Cohen

All rights reserved. No part of this publication may be reproduced or transmitted
in any form or by any means, electronic or mechanical, including photocopying, recording, or any
information storage and retrieval system now known or to be invented, without permission in writing
from the publisher, except by a reviewer who wishes to quote brief passages in connection with a
review written for inclusion in a magazine, newspaper, or broadcast.
The publisher does not have any control over and does not assume any responsibility for author
or third-party websites or their content.

Library of Congress Cataloging-in-Publication Data
Cohen, Tish, date.
The one and only Zoë Lama / by Tish Cohen. — 1st ed.
p. cm.
Summary: Seventh-grader Zoë's status as best advice-giver at Allencroft Middle School is in jeopardy
when sixth-grader Devon Sweeney begins to take over, and until she finds out what is really going on
in Devon's life, Zoë will do just about anything to regain her exalted place in the school hierarchy.
ISBN 978-0-525-47891-1
[1. Competition (Psychology)—Fiction. 2. Interpersonal relations—Fiction. 3. Middle schools—Fiction.
4. Schools—Fiction. 5. Fathers—Fiction.] I. Title.
PZ7.C66474On 2008
[Fic]—dc22   2007028482

Published in the United States by Dutton Children's Books,
a division of Penguin Young Readers Group
345 Hudson Street, New York, New York 10014
www.penguin.com/youngreaders

Designed by IRENE VANDERVOORT

Printed in USA   First Edition
1 3 5 7 9 10 8 6 4 2

For Lucas and Max

Acknowledgments

Warmest thanks go out to: my editors, Stephanie Owens Lurie, at Dutton Children's Books, and Lynne Missen at HarperCollinsCanada. I love working with you both. Sarah Shumway, Irene Vandervoort, and Lisa Adams at Dutton for your support and talent. Iris Tupholme and Charidy Johnson at Harper for believing in Zoë, and Kathryn Wardropper for martinis on the patio. Michael Borum of Etherweave for putting Zoë on the Web. Brett Elmslie for putting the g-ma in Gran. My wonderful literary agent, Daniel Lazar, at Writers House for unwavering support and enthusiasm. Maja Nikolic, also at Writers House, for international efforts. Steve, for handselling this book before it was written. But most of all, Max and Lucas, for teaching me that some things, like snot rockets, never really change.

Contents

The One and Only
Joë Lama

Babies Are a Pain in the Eardrum

I hate going to the doctor. It's total chaos. The entire waiting room is coated with a thin, gluey glaze of mucus. The walls, the receptionist's desk, even the Kleenex box—all sticky. And don't even get me started on the fish tank. The floor is crawling with feverish brats thumping one another with plastic tricycles, and you're never going to find a place to sit, because all the spare seats have spit-up on them.

Nothing against Dr. Jensen, other than the way he sings Beatles songs while he looks into your ear, he's an okay guy for a pediatrician. And if you survive your checkup without wailing, vomiting, or stealing his latex gloves—so you can fill them with water and launch them out your bedroom window later—he gives you an animal cookie on your way out. I don't mind that they aren't chocolate chip cookies. I'm twelve years old, plenty old enough to know it's easier to bribe a blubbering kid with food if it's shaped like an alligator.

I do blame Mrs. Chomsky, his angry receptionist. She just sits in her spinny chair, answering the phone and slapping files on the counter for Dr. Jensen.

Well, it's her lucky day.

I've been home with chicken pox for eight days, twenty-two hours, and thirteen minutes. Not that I'm counting. Dr. Jenkins said, "No school, no friends, no fun." He didn't actually say the no-fun part, but he should have, because I was bored. And major itchy. I knew I had to come for another checkup before I was allowed back in school, so when I wasn't scratching or dreaming about scratching, I was drawing up a diagram for old Mrs. Chomsky. I colored my diagram, labeled it with instructions, and snuck out of the house to get it laminated. (If you ask me, everything in this entire place should be laminated. To make it snot-proof.)

My diagram is based on my one and only rule about babies. I may not have any babies in my family—or any brothers or sisters or fathers, for that matter—but here it is anyway, **Unwritten Rule #15—Babies are a pain in the eardrum, so you better keep them busy while they're waiting to see the doctor.**

My system is based on stations. Keep babies and toddlers moving, don't give them a second to think! Thinking only gets them into trouble, because their heads are still so small. They really only have room for two thoughts: *How loud should I scream?* and *Who can I whack next?* Both of these behaviors are hugely annoying and, as I've mapped out, can be avoided by moving babies from one station to another in three-minute intervals.

You start them off in the Bottle and Juice Station for energy. Then, when the bell rings, they move to the Recreation Station (tricycles) for exercise. Then the bell rings and they move to the Nature Station (fish). After three minutes with their faces glued to the dirty glass, it's over to the Hygiene Station to be scrubbed down with antibacterial wipes. Then three minutes to chew on a book and start all over again.

Simple, really. The mothers do all the work. All Mrs. Chomsky has to do is ring a tiny bell every three minutes and the place should run like spit.

$\mathcal{T}$he moment Dr. Jensen calls my name, I pull out my bell and my diagram—titled "Babypalooza"—and set it

on Chomsky's desk. There. I've done all I can. Like my grandma used to say to me when I was younger, "You can lead a horse to the bathtub, but you can't make her wash behind her ears." Which never even made sense, because after she said it, my mom made me wash behind my ears.

My mother and I follow Dr. Jensen into the examining room. No matter what I'm in for, the drill's always the same. He dances me into the examining room, tells me to take off my shoes, and makes me hold still to get measured. He never bothers to tell me how tall I am—or am *not*—he just scratches something in my file and says, "Not to worry. **What you lack in the size department, you make up for with your gigantic personality!**"

Afterward, he scoops me up onto the examining table and the crinkly paper pokes me hard in the back of my knee.

"And how are our spots today, Miss Zoë Monday Costello?"

Next time I come, I swear, I'm bringing some Wite-Out for that middle name. "Pretty okay." I roll up my sleeves and show him my arms. "Not nearly so spotty."

"I followed all your advice, Dr. Jensen," says my mother

with a tight little smile. "Oatmeal baths, sea-salt baths. Even the tea-tree oil. Just like you said. Dr. Jensen's advice made an enormous difference, didn't it, Zoë?"

"Kind of."

My mother is blushing. She doesn't know I know what I know, but I know it. My mother has a teensy crush on Dr. Jensen. He just thinks she's friendly, but she's not fooling me. She's never *this* friendly.

"Good," he says, pulling out his little flashlight. He looks in my eyes, in my ears, then shoves a Popsicle stick in my mouth. His hair is like an unraveling SOS pad, springing up from his head in every direction. "Say ahhh."

"Ahhh."

"Good." Then he shines his light up my nose and makes a happy grunt. "I see the pustules in your right nostril have dried up nicely."

I don't answer on the grounds that having anything as vile and horrid as "pustules" up my nostril is so embarrassing it takes my words away. I mean, I'm a good person. Sort of. I take care of my mother, my classmates, my teachers, even my grandma, and she doesn't even live with us anymore. I take care of her every Sunday at the Shady Gardens

Home for Seniors by making sure the staff doesn't give her lumpy cocoa. I even take care of the old collie that sleeps under the Shady Gardens nurses' station by filing his toenails and painting them with Mom's favorite nail polish—Midnight Mango.

With all these good works, **I consider gruesome boils inside my innocent nose to be an Act of Hostility on the Part of the Universe.**

"Does your nose feel better?" Dr. Jensen asks me. Loudly.

Trying to ignore him, I sniff and lean down to fake-scratch my ankle, wishing a tornado, a bobcat, or a rashy toddler would burst through the door. Anything to change this sickening subject.

"Zoë?" he says.

"What?"

"Your right nostril. How is it?"

"Umm . . ."

"Zoë, darling, answer Dr. Jensen," says my mom. I can tell by her voice that I'm going to hear about this in the car.

Dr. Jensen looks up my nose again. "Are your pustules causing less discomfort now?"

My pustules? Ugh. I look away, toward a square tin decorated with blue swirls. On the lid, it says BOVINE BALM. "What's that?" I ask.

It works. He looks toward the tin and laughs. "That, Miss Zoë, is a trade secret. My hands get dry and cracked from washing them between patients. I'd heard that this stuff was a miracle moisturizer, so I hunted around for it and what do you think happened?"

I shrug. I really don't know.

"I found it at the drugstore in the lobby downstairs. Only $4.99."

"Four ninety-nine?" squeaks my mother.

"Well, it sounds like you're a man with good economic sense."

Dr. Jensen opens the lid and shows the clear goo to my mother, who pretends she's impressed. I'm thinking it smells like Vaseline, when my mom asks, "Doesn't *bovine* mean for cows?"

Dr. Jensen laughs. "That's why I was surprised to find it at the drugstore. It's made to moisturize the tired, cracked teats of milking cows."

He bends over to write my back-to-school note while my mother rubs the Bovine Balm into her hands. "It does feel marvelous," she says.

He scoops some out. "I bet this stuff is even strong enough to keep my hair in place. Now *that* would be a miracle."

Which gives me an idea.

I have a lot of clients at school. Which is why I have the nickname Zoë Lama. Kids, teachers— even principals—come to me to solve their every problem. And I care about them all, I truly do. But some are just . . . special. Like Sylvia Smye. She's been with me ever since the day in first grade that kids still refer to as "The Great Barrette Disaster." Sylvia's mother tried to tame some of her daughter's cowlicks using yellow ducky barrettes, but by the end of the day, her hair stuck straight up like a horn in the front and Smartin Granitstein started calling her "Unicorn." No matter what I did, I couldn't flatten her hair, so I dug around at the back of my desk for some dusty rubber bands and built myself a horn of my own and then convinced the other girls to do the same.

I've since tried nearly everything to fight Sylvia's cowlicks. Braids, pretty hairbands, scrunchies, clips, and training them by having her wearing a bathing cap to bed for a whole week.

There's really only one thing I haven't tried. My eyes drift over to the little jar of Bovine Balm.

It sure would be good for business, heading back to school with the answer to my very best client's very worst problem. I can just see the kids' faces as Sylvia comes out of the girls' bathroom with smooth, silky hair blowing in the wind and romantic music playing in the background. Everyone would congratulate me for doing the impossible. Everyone would want to know my secret. Even Riley, the Most Unbelievably Cute Guy in School, or MUC-GIS, would stop doubting my meddling. He'd see that my Unwritten Rules can change people's lives. For the better.

Oh, and Sylvia would be happy, too.

Suddenly I can't wait to get back to school.

"Mom?" I smile sweetly, sliding off the end of the exam table. "Can I borrow five dollars?"

She agrees to meet me in the drugstore downstairs, so I head out into the waiting room, which is strangely silent. Sure enough, there's Mrs. Chomsky standing in front of her desk with my bell in her hands.

She rings it and everyone in the room stands up and shifts stations. Mothers are laughing. Babies are gurgling. Toddlers are quiet. Not one single kid is moaning, sniveling, whimpering, or wailing. Mrs. Chomsky notices me in the doorway and mouths, "Thank you."

Another satisfied customer.

*I*t's snowing hard by the time we get back home. Mr. Kingsley, the superintendent, is out front shoveling off the sidewalk so no one falls and sues the building. If you didn't know Mr. Kingsley, you'd think his lumberjack shirt, jeans and work boots, and furry hat with earflaps was a good shoveling uniform. If you did know him, you'd just be thankful a day finally came around that matches his outfit—because that's what he wears every day.

"Good evening, Mr. Kingsley," says my mother. Her arms are full of grocery bags and she can barely see where she's stepping.

He looks up at her and nods, then scowls at me. Grandma caused a little flood a while back and he still suspects me of covering it up. Which I did—who wouldn't cover for their very own grandma? I step over a little mound of snow and give him a smile. "I like your technique, Mr. Kingsley," I say. "Much smarter to shovel length-ways instead of side to side."

I mean it, too. This way he only has to swoop from the front door to the curb and back twice, rather than twenty-five trips from side to side. Saves a lot of energy.

Mom's already swearing at the front door because her key's stuck again. "Mr. Kingsley, are we ever going to get this door fixed?"

"You gotta jiggle it to the right," Mr. Kingsley says. "Like I showed you last time."

"I *am*."

She isn't. "Mom, let me help . . ."

"Shimmy it up and down as you push to the right," he says. "Push hard."

One of her grocery bags slides through her arm and I catch it just before it falls. "Mom, I'll open it."

She jams it harder. "You'd think when rents go up that a person could expect a few repairs." Her face is red as she jiggles her key again.

"Take it up at the next tenants' meeting," Mr. Kingsley says.

She scowls at him and bashes the door with her body.

"Mom . . ."

Finally the door swings open. My mom charges through the lobby and starts stabbing the elevator button. By the time I catch up, she's already stepped inside the car, which smells the exact same as the whole eighth-floor hallway is going to smell. Like Mrs. Grungen's Tuesday-night Golabki. **Hamburger meat, mushrooms, and buckwheat wrapped up in soggy cabbage to look like a dead pigeon wrapped in a greasy napkin.** Which is pretty much how it smells.

Mr. Jeffries gets off as I get on.

He calls back, "Best of luck to you ladies. Elevator's groaning again."

"Terrific," Mom grumbles. She presses 8. Nothing happens. She presses it again. Just as she opens her mouth to swear, sigh, or cluck like Mrs. Chomsky, I whack it hard, right in the center. The doors close and up we go.

She shakes her head. "How *do* you know these things?"

I shrug. "It's what I do."

We stare at the numbers above the doors while the elevator shudders and moans.

"Mom?"

"Yes, dear?"

"You know how you told Dr. Jensen you were so proud of me for barely scratching my pox at all?"

"Yes."

"And you know how he said your daughter won't have one single solitary scar because of her outrageously good behavior?"

Mom smiles. "I don't recall the words *outrageously good* . . ."

"Before I left school, **Mrs. Patinkin said it was my turn to take home the class guinea pig.** It would only be for one weekend and I'd keep him in my room—"

She thinks about it. "There's not a lot of space in the apartment."

"Mom, please!"

"Does he smell?"

"Like sugar cookies! *Please,* Mom!"

"You promise he'd go back on Monday? No excuses?"

I crossed my heart. "Cross my heart."

"Okay."

I squeal and hug her. "Thanks so much. You're going to love Boris."

"Boris?" Mom makes a face. Then she makes her voice all bright and shiny. "So it's back to school with you tomorrow. Back to the old grind."

"I guess."

"You'll have a lot of catching up to do, according to Mrs. Patinkin."

"I know. Annika Pruitt's boyfriend will have forgotten to meet her after school and she'll be 'tragically wounded.' And Stewie Buckenheimer will have lost his third retainer of the year and his parents' dental coverage won't pay for a fourth. And Avery's lips will be cracked right down the middle, because he'll have put his Chap Stick in his front pocket again and it'll have rolled out and gotten lost." I smile.

My mother peers closer at me and squints. "And all this misfortune is a good thing?"

"It's like a rainstorm to an umbrella store," I say with a shrug. "It's good for business. I have a reputation to think of. **If things go well when I'm away, my peoples will figure out they don't need me or my rules. The Zoë Lama could be Ousted.** Overthrown. Usurped."

I never asked to be the maker of all rules. **I started out life as a regular sort of human with an irregular love for chocolate.** It wasn't until I neutralized the school bully back when I was about the size of a toenail that kids began to look to me for guidance.

Suddenly requests poured in for advice. Teachers wanted to know how to keep kindergartners from stuffing carrots up their noses during snack time (play Itsy-Bitsy Spider). Girls wanted to know how to get stains out of party dresses (candle wax and a hot iron) or what to use if they were allergic to sunscreen (diaper-rash cream). Boys wanted to know how to get girls to stop running away from them (throw a scented dryer sheet in with your jeans and tees for long-lasting freshness) and how to get rid of the warts on their thumbs (wrap them in duct tape for ten days).

I became known as the Zoë Lama because people thought of me as a teacher of sorts. And what kind of teacher would I be without a pocketful of Unwritten Rules?

Mom grunts. "You know I don't like you taking pleasure in the distress of others. Even if it is 'good for business.'" She stares at me and one corner of her lip twitches. "Anyway, wherever did you learn a word like *usurped*? I didn't know words like that in seventh grade."

A couple of years ago, I looked up *usurp* **in the dictionary and learned it means to dethrone, seize, or overthrow.** I pull my jacket closed and shiver. "That word haunts me every day of my life."

There'll Be No Stepping Up in My Absence. None.

Crud.

I stop dead in my tracks and look around the property of Allencroft Middle School, my breath puffing out in little clouds. The place is full of ice and empty of kids. Which makes total sense, since the 8:40 bell has already rung. What did I expect . . . that people would stand outside in the snow, risking late slips and frostbite, because this just *might* be the day I return from quarantine?

It's not like I expected a welcome sign out here. I'm not an idiot. Besides, everyone knows that tape doesn't stick in the cold. The sign would blow away in about three seconds. Quickly, I scan the bushes at the edge of the school fence. Hmm. Nothing but snow and lost mittens.

I got up super early this morning so I could load up my backpack and get here before the bell. But halfway to school I realized I forgot my doctor's note. And my binder. And my pencil case. So I had to go back home, and now I'm late. What I didn't forget is the following:

1) Antibacterial wipes so I can disinfect my desktop—in case anything fungus-y or festering touched it while I was in exile.

2) A red apple for Brianna Simpson, because the skin contains Quercetin, which should make her sneeze less around Boris the guinea pig.

3) A baggie full of chocolate chips for my #1 and #2 BFIS (Best Friends in School) Susannah Barnes and Laurel Sterling. I'll save just a few so I can bribe Smartin Granitstein not to pour grape juice in his ear at lunchtime. That's one delight I did not miss.

4) A Wundercloth we got in the mail that's supposed to de-smudge the smudgiest glasses. Avery Buckner's smeary glasses could very well be the eighth wonder of the world, and should make a nice test subject.

5) Bovine Balm. For my #1 BCIS (Best *Client* in School) Sylvia.

If I want to see anyone before class starts, I'd better hurry. I tear across the snowy field with my schoolbag bashing against my knees and cold wind biting at my face.

*T*he first thing that hits me inside the building is the smell of school. I suck in a deep breath and smile. Ahh, there's nothing quite like it. Photocopies, pencils, winter jackets, and floor cleaner, all mixed into one.

Bloomer Girl, aka fifth-grader Allegra Lohman, rushes past. Not only are her boots looking freshly buffed, but her backward haircut (long in front, short in back) seems to be turned right-way-round. Which isn't remotely possible. Hair doesn't grow that fast. "Hey, Allegra," I call after her. "I'm back!"

She spins around. "Huh?" **For one ugly moment, she seems to not recognize me.** Then she smiles and says, "Oh yeah. How was Florida?"

Florida? "No, I was sick. Deathly ill. I had the chicken pox, remember?"

"Um, sort of . . ."

"I was in quarantine. Total lockdown . . ."

But she's already gone.

The farther in I go, the more I realize something's not right. Brianna's down the hall and I can see from here she has good color in her cheeks—her freckles are barely noticeable—and could that be . . . ? I stop and squint. It is! The most vile boy in the school, Smartin Granitstein, is carrying an armload of actual library books.

I turn a corner to come face-to-face with Susannah and Laurel, who are talking to three girls from sixth grade. Susannah is my #1 BFIS for being fierce loyal and for being almost-but-not-quite famous. Famous enough from her TV commercials to need to wear dark glasses everywhere, but not famous enough that we get driven to the movies in her limo. Mostly because she doesn't have one. Yet. And my #2 BFIS, Laurel, well, how can you not love Laurel? She only eats blue food, and she makes us laugh. Mostly at her, but she's cool with that.

As I run over to them, the three Sixer girls scatter. Susannah and Laurel squeal and rush to hug me so hard they pick me up.

"Zoë!" says Susannah from behind her big sunglasses. "You're back from the dead! Wait . . ." She backs up and lowers her glasses, but only for a split second. "You're not contagious, are you?"

"Nope." I beam.

Laurel sneers at Susannah. "Worried

what a couple of scabs might do to your acting career?"

"As a matter of fact, yes! **One scar and my agent would drop me like an overheated latte.** You think I'll land that Neutrogena commercial with bumpy skin?"

For Susannah, who up until this point has only done commercials for bed-wetting, sanitary pads, and head lice, landing a commercial where she gets to stand at a sink and splash sparkling clean water on her glowing skin is pretty much The Ultimate.

"Whatever," says Laurel, who seems to be still battling that troublesome zit on her chin. She pulls her blue turtleneck up to her mouth and smiles at me. "Good to have you back!"

"It was SO boring, sitting around watching *Regis and Kelly* every day," I say. "Plus, I had to entertain little kids all the time. My mother's friends kept bringing their darlings over for free babysitting so they wouldn't have to haul drooling, wailing toddlers around the grocery store."

Susannah crinkles her nose in disgust. "But you were contagious!"

I nod. "Exactly what I said. But, apparently, they'd all been vaccinated."

"Bummer," says Laurel.

"Exactly what I said."

I unzip my schoolbag and pick through my supplies. "But I'm back and I'm prepared to fix everybody who broke while I was gone. I have a nail buffer for Boris's split toenail, mints for Mrs. Patinkin—ever since she switched to decaf coffee, her breath hasn't been the same . . ." I stop talking because Susannah and Laurel are nudging each other. "What?"

"Nothing," says Susannah, fidgeting with her zipper. "We'd better get to class. The bell's going to ring."

"Forget class. Why do you guys look all nervous?"

Laurel nudges Susannah. "Tell her."

"You tell her!"

Laurel says, "It's just that things aren't nearly as bad as you think around here."

I narrow my eyes. "How not nearly so bad?"

"Things are actually good. *Really* good," says Laurel.

"But how can that be?" I ask, feeling my nostrils flare. "I've been gone for a week and a day."

Susannah twists her mouth to one side. **"Remember Devon Sweeney—the Sixer?"**

"No."

"You wouldn't. Before you left, she was a total dork. She hung out with the Emos behind the baseball diamond and wrote poems about her dead cat."

"What do I care about Devon and her lousy cat?"

Laurel shifts her books to her left arm. "Because, **while you were gone, she stepped up.**"

Huh?

Susannah nods. "It's true. It's like you never left. She kind of took over."

"It started when Annika Pruitt was having one of her 'tragically wounded' moments," says Laurel. "She found out that Justin had Meredith Morgan's phone number written on the bottom of his shoe. The very last number was worn off, but still, Annika could tell. She locked herself in a bathroom stall and Devon found her. She talked Annika off the ledge."

I shake my head. "What ledge? You said she was in the bathroom."

"The toilet ledge. Annika was about to dunk Justin's history binder."

"She should have," I say. "Justin's got a history. A bad one."

"Devon said all she needed to do was fluff up her hair—" Susannah explains.

I interrupt. "She told Annika to fluff up all that hair? Right there in the stall? That's not even sanitary. Annika's hair is bigger than Justin's ego!"

"But it worked," says Laurel. "Justin's a sucker for curls. By that afternoon, he was following Annika around like he was on a leash."

I'm so mad I catch my finger while zipping up my bag. Annika's always been a loyal client of mine. So has her enormo-hair. I've coached it through everything from seriously nasty bangs to an even nastier home perm. Any and all hair advice comes from me and her overworked hairstylist.

The second bell rings. I march toward Mrs. Patinkin's homeroom. Susannah and Laurel jog to catch up.

"Zoë, don't be upset," says Susannah. "Think of it as a good thing. Devon's saved you tons of work. Now you can relax and focus on catching up with your schoolwork. And us. Mostly us." She giggles.

"She moved in on my turf," I say.

"For a few days . . . and now that you've returned she can go back to her rotten poetry," says Laurel with a wave of her hand. **"Don't worry. You're still the One and Only Lama in this school."**

I give my girls the secret punch for believing in me, which comes from the knuckles and involves an unexpected maneuver at the end. But if I told you any more, I'd have to kill you.

Just before I reach the classroom, I'm picked up and twirled around from behind. Which is annoying when you're as small as me, because it's been happening to you ever since you learned to crawl. I turn around and insta-smile because the annoying picker-upper isn't annoying after all. **It's Riley Sinclair, the Most Unbelievably Cute Guy in School (MUCGIS) and the boy I'm going to marry,** and he's wearing the shirt I gave him for his birthday.

"Hi," I say, because his cuteness has temporarily blurred my thoughts.

"Zozers!" he says. If anyone other than Riley called me this, I'd thump them. But Riley gets extra-special privileges, for obvious reasons. "How much did you miss me?"

I hold up my finger and thumb real close together to show him I only missed him about a half inch, and he fake-dies a painful death, like I've stabbed him in the rugby shirt . . . which I'd never do on account of liking both him and his shirt way too much.

Mrs. Patinkin raps a ruler against her desk. "Take your seats, people."

I start to follow Riley inside, when Susannah grabs my arm and pulls me back. "There she is!" She's pointing down the empty hallway.

"Who?"

"Devon Sweeney. Did you see her?"

I shake my head. "All I saw was a flash of glossy blond hair."

Susannah nods. "Exactly."

$\mathcal{I}$'m watching the clock in science class. It's nearly 3:15 and I still haven't gotten more than a glimpse of this Devon Sweeney from behind. Although, I've heard enough about her to rot me from the inside out:

Avery Buckner said, "Zoë, Devon's like an angel!"

Sylvia Smye, after slipping the Bovine Balm into her bag, said, "Have you seen her legs, Zoë? They're as long as a colt's!"

And Riley, who's never really approved of my chocaholic-ism, said, "She hasn't eaten a speck of sugar in three years, Zoë. Can you imagine? **She's your polar opposite!**"

Polar opposite, my elbow. My legs may be shorter than a colt's eyelashes, and I'd rather be ripped apart by wolverines than go off chocolate chips for even three days, but I'm definitely an-gelic. If you ask the right person.

It seems I'm doomed to just miss Devon. Every time I enter a class-room, gym, cafeteria, or stairwell, she's just left. The only evidence of Devon Sweeney's existence I came across all day was an efficient blond bob disappearing through a doorway, a dropped pen-cil with teeth marks in it (I'd *never* gnaw on an instrument of higher learning!), and an empty bag of veggie puffs in the cafeteria trash.

Words Made of Churning Bubbles of Intestinal Gases Are Not Words. They're Sewage.

Wednesday morning I'm sitting at my wobbly desk at the back of the class, trying desperately to ignore the vomitous haze of stink forming above Smartin's wet boots on my left, and Alice Marriott's prancing kitten barrettes and matching socks, which are soiling up the atmosphere on my right. It's even less simple to ignore the crumbly stuff behind Avery's ears, since he sits right in front of me. It's something of a soap-scum biohazard and I'm finding it hard to look away.

Up at the front of the class, where the sun shines brighter and the air quality is better, Maisie and Brianna giggle over something in Brianna's desk. Susannah and Laurel style each other's hair. Riley shoots rubber bands into the trash can. And Tall Paul and Small Paul compare shoe sizes. Sigh. I miss my Frontie days.

A couple of months ago, I returned from hauling Smartin to the office for solitary confinement, and found a new girl sitting at my desk. Maisie. It seemed she needed to sit right up front with Laurel, Susannah, and Riley. Something to do with her depth-perception problem. So, just like that, she took my place among the Fronties and I was cruelly shipped to the rear to fend for myself in the slimy underworld of the Backies.

So here I sit, tiny warrior that I am.

To take my mind off Avery's ears, I stare at Sylvia. Dear sweet Sylvia, not quite a Frontie, not quite a Backie. Just sitting in the nether region of the middle—always without a complaint. She truly is my dream client. She works exclusively with my advice and almost never double-checks with her mother. She keeps her expectations realistic. Knows no amount of advice is going to turn her into Susannah Barnes. And, she doesn't expect success to happen overnight.

Honestly, **I see Sylvia as a little bird who's fallen out of the nest too early.** Her feathers still poke out in every which direction (cowlicks), her little wings make her practically defenseless (total lack of muscle tone), and every so often there's a worm in her beak (lettuce in her braces).

I watch as she pecks hopelessly at something in her

binder. She pulls her hand away and accidentally yanks out her timetable, tearing the three little holes in the paper. For a moment, she stares at the shredded holes. She seems to slump, and her little beak tilts up toward the sky.

I dig through the office-supplies section of my desk. "Sylvia," I whisper. She spins around and smiles. I toss her a small package of stick-'em hole-fixing thingies. I watch the plastic box sail through the air and realize, too late, that Sylvia's holding her hands too far apart to catch it. The pack drops to the floor. It bursts open and tiny O's scatter far and wide across the room.

Like tiny grubworms. Or maybe ringworms, because they're round. Or tapeworms, because they're sticky.

Just as Sylvia is picking them up, in walks Mrs. Patinkin with none other than Mr. Renzetti, our principal.

Mrs. Patinkin looks at the mess and blushes at Mr. Renzetti, who is pulling a sticky white ring from the bottom of his expensive-looking shoe. When Mrs. Patinkin sees this, her eyes bug. She says as calm as she can, "Sylvia Smye, I'll ask you to keep your school supplies in your desk, not on the floor!"

"But they're not—" chirps Sylvia.

"Sylvia," the teacher says with a fake smile, "just pick them up."

I put up my hand. "Actually, Mrs. Patinkin, it's my fault. I threw them at Sylvia and the stupid box exploded, and then, like, ten thousand holey things flew out and—"

"Thank you for your candor and frankness, Zoë. After Mr. Renzetti leaves, I'll ask you to write both of these qualities on the board and we'll study them." She looks at Mr. Renzetti. "I always like to reinforce vocabulary. If they can just learn to employ their verbiage in the real world, they'll be that much better prepared—"

Mr. Renzetti looks up at the clock. "Can we get started here? I have a meeting in twenty minutes."

Mrs. Patinkin practically bows. "Class, Mr. Renzetti has an announcement to make. Put down your pencils and listen."

One of Mr. Renzetti's shoes makes a sticky noise as he walks to the front of the room, but he pretends not to notice. He smiles. "Good morning, everybody. I've got some good news and some better news. What would you like to hear first?"

About a hundred hands shoot up in the air and everyone says, "Ooh, ooh, ooh!" Small Paul is practically bouncing out of his seat and Smartin's hand is stretched so far out, his fingertips are officially Fronties.

"The better news!" grunts Smartin.

"No!" Avery spins around. "The *good* news always comes first!"

"You wouldn't know good news if it bit you in the lip," whispers Smartin. "You'd never see it coming through those greasy glasses!"

"Boys," says Mrs. Patinkin. She's glaring.

"How about we have a rock, paper, scissors contest?" asks Alice. "Starting with me and Zoë. Winner fights Martin. And that winner fights Avery. And that winner chooses the news."

I've said it before and I'll say it again. **It's a moron colony back here.**

"Thank you, Alice," says Mr. Renzetti. "But, in the interest of saving time, I'll just go ahead with the good news."

Avery clenches his dirty fist and hisses, *"Yes!"*

Mr. Renzetti looks toward the door like he's planning his escape. "Mrs. Peebles, one of our sixth-grade teachers, is leaving the school. She and her family will be moving to Oregon next week, where she will finally achieve her lifelong dream of becoming principal of a very prominent private school. Allencroft Middle School couldn't be more proud of our very own Mrs. Peebles." He pauses a moment to make sure we look proud enough, but we pretty much look like our usual selves. So he continues, "Unfortunately, this means that her triplets, Dara, Lara, and Melanie, will no longer be part of our sixth-grade community. And when a school our size loses its very favorite set of triplets, it creates something of a numerical imbalance."

Mrs. Patinkin hurries and writes *numerical,* then *imbalance,* on the blackboard for us to torture ourselves over later. Great.

As Mr. Renzetti continues, a bunch of scraping and rustling comes from the hallway. "Now we get to the better part. Half of Mrs. Peebles's class will be absorbed by the other sixth-grade class."

Harrison Huxtable's hand shoots up.

"Yes, Harrison?"

"When you say they're absorbing the kids, do you mean it subliminally? Like when a commercial flashes Cokes at you zillions of times and I can't figure out why I'm thirsty?"

The class giggles and snorts.

"Shut up!" I cough a classwide warning into my hand. Harrison might be bulkier than the rest of us, pound for pound, but that just means he deserves *more* respect, not less.

Mrs. Patinkin writes *subliminally* on the board and

Mr. Renzetti smiles. "No. It means **half of the sixth-grade class will move into the other sixth-grade class.** Effective today."

Up goes Laurel's hand. Quickly, I pour chocolate chips onto my desk to reward her. She got "satisfactory" for class participation on her last report card, so any kind of effort deserves to be noticed. Laurel asks, "What happens to the other half of Mrs. Peebles class? Are they going to Oregon, too?"

Mr. Renzetti smiles. "No. They're being absorbed by another class. A seventh-grade class with very small numbers . . ."

"Ooh, ooh!" Brianna says, her hand waggling in the air. Renzetti looks about ready to retire. "Yes, Brianna?"

"What about the empty classroom? Has anyone decided what to use it for? Because some schools in California have meditation rooms."

"I'm afraid we haven't begun to plan—"

LameWizard Richard looks up from his hobgoblin GameWizard like he's just noticed there are humans on the planet, and says, "Maybe it could be a video-game room. Like a social gathering place."

"As I mentioned," Mr. Renzetti continued, "we haven't yet allocated our extra space."

"So then where are the leftover kids going?" asks Harrison Huxtable.

"Right here," says Mr. Renzetti with his chest all puffed up. **"As of this minute, you're officially a six/ seven split class."**

"Your *face* is a six/seven split class," mumbles Smartin.

Mr. Renzetti looks around, confused. "Did somebody say something?"

Everyone looks at Smartin, then the door flies open. A bunch of Sixers file in, each one pushing a grubby metal desk and chair. Mrs. Patinkin claps her hands and shouts, "Will my Sevens from the back of the class please slide your desks up into the empty spaces between the front desks?"

You don't have to ask me twice. Before the words are out of her mouth, I've got my backpack and chair piled on top of my desk and I'm shoving the whole thing up front. I don't stop until I'm settled right between Susannah and Laurel and directly in front of Riley, so he can't get me out of his mind.

This is shaping up to be the very best Wednesday ever.

My Frontie status has *finally* been restored! At the exact same time, Susannah and Laurel give me our secret punch for joy. It's rarely used because the level of joy I'm feeling after my chicken-pox exile *and* Backie exile doesn't come around too often. This punch involves the heel of the hand and a dainty whoop sound. But that's all I'm at liberty to say.

We turn around and watch the Sixers, all of whom are depressingly taller than me, slide their desks to the back, where they belong. One Sixer burps out a hello—and I pray I'm mistaken, but it sounded like a girl—and a couple of Sixer boys snort and scratch themselves like baboons.

Ugh.

At recess, I'll have to issue these immature vulgarians a couple of rules. Starting with **Unwritten Rule # 17,** which I'm just this minute inventing. **Words Made of Churning Bubbles of Intestinal Gases Are Not Words. They're Sewage.**

After Mr. Renzetti leaves, Mrs. Patinkin gets the vulgarians settled then makes a big deal about stapling together the two class lists. So now we have to sit through double the number of lousy names after announcements. She reads our names first, as she should, and when she flips her page and starts calling the Sixer names, we all giggle and look at one another. What were these Sixer parents thinking?

Pilar Bliss?

Lettice Weatherhead?

Cheever Duff?

The names just keep getting worse and worse, until finally Mrs. Patinkin finishes and puts her list into the attendance folder. I'm digging out chocolate chips for my new neighbors, when a singsongish voice calls from the back, "Mrs. Patinkin? You forgot me."

Mrs. Patinkin opens her folder and scans the names. "Oops. I'm sorry. And you are?"

I turn around in my chair. A proud-looking blond girl is arranging a cupful of sharpened pencils on her desk. **She flicks something off her pink cardigan and says, "I'm Devon Sweeney."**

*M*y mother always tells me it's rude to stare. So I'm trying really hard not to. Correction, I'm trying really hard not to let anyone see me stare. I have this shiny chrome lip-gloss container I keep in my schoolbag, and if I hold it at just the right angle, I can see everything Devon does. The way she licks the tip of each pencil before she writes. The way she gathers her eraser shavings into a tidy little pile then sweeps them into a Ziploc baggie. The way she tucks her well-behaved hair behind her ears over and over so not one single hair ever gets the chance to roam free.

Then Laurel jabs me in the ribs and I look up. Mrs. Patinkin is waiting for me to answer some question I didn't hear. She is pointing to the words *This week's keeper of the pig* on the blackboard.

"I know you've been waiting for a chance to watch Boris for months now, Zoë. And this would have been your scheduled turn."

Would have been?

Mrs. Patinkin continues, "It's just that I've had a rather special request from one of our new classmates. Devon has a very important weekend planned and wants to bring Boris home to help her celebrate. Devon, why don't you come to the front of the class and tell everyone your exciting news."

I make a shocked face at Susannah. **Devon getting Boris is an Indescribable Indignation.** Which means it's crazy annoying.

Susannah huffs out loud in agreement. You gotta love Susannah.

Devon swishes her skirt as she makes her way to the front. Then she spins around and smiles way too sweetly. Her cheeks turn all pink. "This is *so* embarrassing," she says, and everyone giggles in sympathy. "I'm getting my black belt in karate this Saturday. There's a big presentation where I have to chop a piece of wood in half and perform in front of a panel of tons of people. Anyway, my parents are making this huge, insane deal out of it and asked what I wanted for my gift." A piece of blond hair falls down against her perfect chin and she tucks it back in place. "They were thinking I'd ask for an iPod or a portable CD player." She laughs and crosses one coltish leg in front of the other. "But all I really wanted was to bring home my new homeroom-class guinea pig for the weekend."

Her class guinea pig? She's only been in the class for about fifty-five seconds! Who's the one who's been feeding him, watering him, changing his cedar shavings all year? Putting in his eyedrops when he scratched his cornea on a jagged piece of timothy grass? Trimming his toenails? Me, that's who.

I put up my hand to ask the question that, I'm sure, is on

everyone's mind. "Devon, what happens if you don't break the board in half? I mean, what if you crush your hand, or wake up Saturday morning with food poisoning or chicken pox?"

The whole class is silent. Mrs. Patinkin's smiles melts down her face.

Devon tilts her head. "My dad says that's the thing about me. Once I set my mind on something, I don't let *anything* stop me."

Mrs. Patinkin claps her hands. "Well then, it's all settled. Boris will spend the weekend at Devon's house."

Devon kind of bows; then, on her way back to her desk, she stops at Boris's cage to pick him up and nuzzle him. Holding his brown, white, and black body in her palms, she kisses him on the nose. Then Boris lets out this happy little squeak—the kind of squeak he only ever makes when he hears a carrot being cracked in half—and the whole class goes, "Awww."

Even Mrs. Patinkin!

The Missing Link Is
Not So Missing Anymore

When the recess bell rings, the Sixers barrel out of the class like savages. Doesn't surprise me. I have a theory about Sixers. Anyone under the age of seventh grade has not yet developed the part of their brain that turns them into actual human beings. They still don't know enough to shower more than once a week, only half of them look like they've ever held a brush, and, if it's raining, you can be sure that almost every Sixer will show up soaked to the knees from puddle-stomping.

According to my science textbook, in the theory of evolution, scientists believe there's a missing link between fish and land animals. Which means that when early fishy lifeforms finally swam to the surface and looked around, wishing they could crawl out onto the beach and lie in the sun to dry out their pruney skin, some kind of half-fish, half-land animal should have evolved before actual land animals did. That missing creature is the missing link. But I don't think it's missing at all. I think the missing link is Sixers.

I watch Smartin pull off his shoes, sniff his wet socks, and tug on his sopping boots. He stomps out, making sickening squishing noises with each step.

I sigh. Of course there's a chance I'm wrong. **The missing link could very well be Smartin Granitstein.**

As I pull on my boots, I feel a timid little tap on my shoulder. It's Sylvia.

"Hi, Zoë. Do you have a minute?"

See what I mean about the perfect-client thing? Sylvia doesn't make it all about her. It's all about *me* first, then, sometime later, we get to her. I like that.

"Sure," I say. "Sorry about the holey stickers exploding."

She tucks her chin into her shoulder and smiles. "That's okay." She holds up a sticker-covered shoe. "They actually look good on my sneakers."

They don't, but I fake-nod to boost her self-esteem. I ask, "Did you get my e-mails while I was gone? About not using plastic in the microwave and taking the other route to school?"

"Yup. I cut through the townhouse parking lot, like you

said, and I got to school two and a half minutes earlier. Now I have time to stop in front of Brandon's house and see if I can see him through the bushes."

No. Spying on your crush is very bad. Especially if your crush is Brandon Skinner, Lord of the LameWizards—Allencroft Middle School's gaggle of electronic gamers. "Actually, Sylvia . . ." I put my arm around her shoulders and guide her into the hall before Laurel and Susannah go outside and get involved in some sort of horrid winter sport in the playground. "You might want to put those extra minutes to better use. Like getting to class early enough to comb your bangs after pulling off your hat. You know what static cling does to thin hair . . ."

She nods furiously as we jog down the stairs to the foyer. "Right. That's true. But he actually waved at me when he was getting into his mom's Jeep last Thursday."

I stop her. "There'll be no more hedge-hiding for you. No amount of waving is worth the scratches and scrapes on your face. Or your pride."

"But I'm waiting for the chance to ask him to my Scottish dance recital."

Whoa. "I'd rethink that one," I say, holding the door

open. Wind nearly blows off her hat and she grabs it.

"But why?" she asks. "I happen to know his ancestors are Scottish and Devon said—"

"What?"

Sylvia looks flustered. It's so noisy in the playground, I can barely hear her.

"Well, I know *one* of his grandparents is from Scotland, anyway. Two of the others are from Ireland, but it's still pretty close . . ."

From a snowbank, Laurel shouts, "Zoë, come see this!"

I wave to her that I'll be a minute. "No, you said something about Devon."

"Oh yeah. Just that she said I should get front-row tickets for Brandon and tell him I'll leave a chocolate caramel on his seat."

This makes my eyes clamp shut in horror. **Unwritten Rule #4—One Lama Per School.** No Exceptions—exists for a reason. Two lamas lead to a sticky, gooey mess. "No, no, no. That's terrible advice!"

"She said it was romantic. Like something from a Hilary Duff movie."

"It's sappy and needy and . . . tragic!" I say, rubbing my forehead. "It's not for real life. I don't recommend you try that with any boy, but *especially* not a boy like Brandon."

"Why? **Devon says his long eyelashes mean he's passionate.**"

I roll my eyes. I swear I'm never going into quarantine again. "Long eyelashes mean he has *dust allergies.* Brandon has a long, ugly history of not wanting girls that want him bad."

She crinkles her nose. "I've never heard that."

"Of course you haven't heard it. That's what you have me for. Don't you remember last Valentine's Day, when Alice sent Brandon a cookiegram that said, 'Roses are red, violets are blue, buttercups have sunshine, and I have you'?"

"No."

"He sent back a broken piece of cookie that said, 'My dad's a cop.'"

Sylvia looks sick. "Whoa."

"Whoa is right. **The only way to land Brandon Skinner is to shatter his core first.** Nothing horrible, just enough to make him think you couldn't care less about him. Then, and only then, you can think about inviting *someone else* to your dance recital right in front of him."

"Another boy?"

"Sure. Or a girlfriend." I reach down to smooth my scarf. "Someone who helps you out from time to time . . ."

Sylvia gets knocked sideways by a couple of sixth-grade boys having a snowball fight. She rights herself and adjusts her hat. "I already asked. Devon's busy that day."

"I meant me!" I squeak.

"Oh! I'd love to have you there. I just figured you might have rules about going to client events and stuff."

I thump my fist above my heart, then start walking backward toward Laurel and Susannah. "For my best clients, I make exceptions."

I catch up with the girls, who are stopping kids from trampling something that's been written in the snow. It says:

ZC
+
RS

I look around and see RS lurking in the bushes, grinning. His friends are teasing him. I give him a smile. Hedge-hiding might not be allowed for Sylvia. Ever. But a boy as cute as Riley spying from the cedar bushes is definitely allowed. If he's staring at me, that is.

There Is No Excuse for Guys Named Thunder Who Stand on Windy Cliffs

The next evening, I'm lying on my bed studying for my French test, and thinking *caniche* doesn't really sound like it should mean "poodle" in French. It sounds more like some sort of greasy pastry filled with duck meat and walnuts. Just when I'm realizing France messed up poodles' reputations even more by inventing that crazy pom-pom haircut, a warbling sound comes from my computer. An instant message!

I race to my computer hoping it's from Riley. But it isn't.

g-ma: yo zo ☺

I stare at the message, trying to figure out who g-ma is. Could it be Gina Mercer from health class? I answer . . .

zoelama: heeeyyyy
g-ma: met qt @ bingo

Bingo? What kind of seventh-grader plays bingo? Even more curious—since when are cute guys at bingo?

> zoelama: ?name?
> g-ma: ♥Fritz♥

Good grief. It's worse than I thought. This is exactly why I discourage my clients from running around bingo halls. They're drafty, crowded, and full of gamblers and boys named Fritz.

> g-ma: he likes cigars

Gross!

> zoelama: gina—I no Rodney broke yor ♥ last year but u cant lower yorself like ths. Unwritn Rool #20 clearly st8s: Smokng is Despcble and Loathesm.
> g-ma: ?whoz gina?
> zoelama: U!!
> g-ma: Im GRANDMA!
> zoelama: grandma? wat r u doing online?
> g-ma: rofl, signed up 4 a class—Seniors on Surf-boards

I try to imagine Grandma sitting at a keyboard in her flowered housecoat and curlers.

g-ma: g2g . . . nos!!
zoelama: ?nos?
g-ma: nurse over shoulder!

I sit back in my chair, stunned. *My* **grandma**, who's only been in Shady Gardens Home for Seniors for a month, **has turned into some kind of instant-messaging hipster** who picks up cigar-smoking, gambler boys named Fritz. And she calls herself g-ma!

The thing about Grandma is—she has Alzheimer's. Which sometimes makes her do and say some pretty wild stuff. But now that she's in a special home, Mom and I know she's safe. So . . . maybe it's not such a bad thing that she's having a bit of fun. What's the worst that can happen? That her curlers start to stink from Fritz's cigar smoke? Suddenly I'm happy for her. My grandma is getting a life.

And, other than the g-ma part, it's kind of cool that Grandma is IMing, since I've missed being able to ask her for advice. Like with this whole Devon thing—Grandma is about the only one who would know exactly how to make me feel better.

zoelama: Grandma? U ther?

zoelama: g-ma?

She's gone.

"Aagh!" My mother wails from the kitchen.

I tear out of my room to find her on her hands and knees, beating the linoleum floor with our dish scrubber. "Bugs!" she says. "A whole revolting family of them."

I look back into the hall to see a small brown insect with a shiny shell crawl out from under the wall. He stops and acts confused—like he expected to be someplace else and is disappointed—then wiggles his antenna thingies at me. Before my mother sees him and scrubs him to death, I try to poke him back under the wall. But I guess he likes what he sees in our apartment, because every time I poke at him, he runs around my finger so he can get back into the room. He scoots right past my sock and zooms—

WHACK!

That's the thing about bugs—they never listen.

"I'm telling you, this building is falling apart!" Mom says. "The elevator, the front door, the incinerator, and now roaches?" She looks at me like I should have an answer.

But all I have is a question. "What's wrong with the incinerator?"

She murders another bug. "There's something stuck in the chute. I have to go down to the fifth floor to dump our trash or it gets stuck. This never would have happened when your father was around, I can tell you that much!"

I scoot closer and drop down onto my knees. **Stories about my father,** who died before I turned five, **are pretty much my favorite thing in the world.** "Why? Were roaches scared of him?"

"No. But he'd have made sure the owner did a better job of running this building. And if things didn't improve, he'd make sure we moved someplace else. Like when we moved here. Our last apartment had walls so thin we could hear our neighbors snoring. It kept me up all night, so your dad found us this place. And do you know what sold him on it?"

"Thicker walls?"

She smashes a bug, then smiles. "Well, that was one thing. But it was very important to your father that you be able to see Hunter's Park from your bedroom window. You didn't want to move from our old place because you were madly in love with the little French boy down the hall. He used to wear a powder-blue sweater with a woolly elephant on the front and pom-poms on the shoulders. Anyway, we couldn't afford a place really close to the park, but your dad made sure that when you looked west, you could see a nice sliver of greenery peeking out from between the buildings."

"Really?"

"Absolutely. You were the number one most important thing in the world to your dad."

If you have to miss a dad, it would be easier if he was a dad who thought you were, say, the third most important thing in the world. Or even the second. Knowing he loved you that much is kind of like torture. You know everything you do for the rest of your life would have been better with him around. How could it not? I mean, even if I *was* in love with a little French boy with bad taste in sweaters, moving here must have been so much easier because of that sliver of green. Which makes my stomach queasy.

"He would never want you to grow up like this. With groaning elevators and bugs."

"I didn't hear the bugs groaning."

Mom puts her hands on her hips and shoots me an exasperated look.

My stomach kind of flutters. "We're not moving, are we?"

"Sadly, no. We can't afford a place better than this." She stomps down on another bug, but—lucky for the bug—she misses. The bug scoots under the oven. "Listen, I'm expecting my book club any minute and I'm going to need your help." She hands me the dish scrubber, which has brown roach guts in the bristles and I hope is going into the trash. "You are going to have to be on duty. I do not want my friends to know we have bugs, so *please* kill them quietly. And whatever you do, don't let any roaches crawl into the living room."

$\mathcal{H}$alf an hour later, I'm parked on the kitchen floor with my homework spread out on the floor in front of me. But I'm making absolutely no progress because I have the dish scrubber in one hand and the phone in the other.

"So then . . ." Susannah says with her mouth full. I don't have to ask what she's eating. She just got back from her agent Sammy's office, which happens to be right above the best donut shop in the city. "Then Sammy tells me that if I get this Neutrogena facewash commercial, I'll have weight."

Huh? "Because of the donuts?" I smack the floor and frighten a bug, who takes off under the fridge.

"No. I'll have power. Clout. He says if I land this ad, he'll bump me up to actress. Not just model. He'll send me out on auditions for TV shows, movies, you know. Big stuff."

"Wow. You could hang with Hollywood brats instead of regular brats like me and Laurel. Hang on a sec . . ." From the living room, I can hear my mother and her book-club ladies swooning. I peer around the corner to see Susannah's mother holding up the cover of her book, which has a muscley, long-haired guy standing on a cliff with his shirt half blown off. Which is weird, because I always thought book-club people read classic books, like *Tom Sawyer* or *Pride and Prejudice*. **I've never heard of book clubs picking books like** *Thunder's Passions*. All the ladies study their covers, which are exactly the same, and start saying things like:

"No, I bet he does ab crunches," and

"Oh, he definitely uses a cross-trainer. You can tell by his core!" and

"I'm looking, I'm looking."

"Sus?" I whisper into the phone. "Our mothers have seriously lost it. Did you see their crummy book?"

Susannah laughs. "Yeah. The guy on the cover is a total doof. Come on, his name is Thunder!"

"And why is he all oily?"

"I actually don't mind the oil. It makes his muscles pop."

"I guess so. But what's with his shirt? You can't tell me it was made without buttons. Or that the wind is so strong it ripped them off. I seriously hope when we're old we never get this desperate—"

There's a big gasp in the other room. I peek again and right away see the problem. **A very large bug,** maybe the grandfather of all the other cockroaches, **is crawling over the toe of the very fanciest lady's shoe.** I drop the phone onto the floor with a clatter, and tear into the living room. All of the women freeze as they watch the roach crawl past the other feet and veer back toward the kitchen. No one says a word.

I quickly scoop him up in my hands and laugh. "Oops! My science project is escaping!" Just as I scoot the heck out of there, my mother catches my eye and mouths, "Thank you."

Then I hear her say, "Sorry, Lorraine."

*W*hen the ladies finally leave, I'm still on the phone with Susannah, who is worrying because Friday is pizza lunch at school and she can't afford to get a pimple from pepperoni grease. As Susannah lists all the horrible healthy crap she plans to bring for lunch instead, I watch Lorraine slip my mother a business card. "Call me," she says, laying her hand over my mom's.

My mother stares at the card, confused.

Lorraine asks, "Have you considered moving?"

"Are you kidding?" my mom says. "Only every day of my life. But I seriously doubt I could afford much better."

Lorraine winks. "Call me. Housing prices have really dropped. You might be surprised at what you can afford."

And, just like that, my mother stuffs the business card into her pocket!

My heart pounds faster. We can never move. For one thing, I've lived in this building almost my entire life. For another thing, it's close to school and friends and Gram's hipster nursing home. I mean, me and Gram have to stay in touch—she only moved out of our apartment and into

Shady Gardens Home for Seniors a few weeks ago. Besides, she might need help with her instant messaging!

A little wildlife isn't so terrible . . . it's charming. Earthy. Organic.

Susannah's voice drones on. ". . . but then again, cranberry juice might stain my teeth and my mother says I'm not allowed to use those whitening strips again until I'm twenty, because of hazardous chemicals. What do you think?"

My mother says good-bye to her friends and shuts the door.

"Zoë?"

Mom pulls Lorraine's card out of her pocket again and examines it, then wanders toward her bedroom with a dreamy look on her face.

"Zoë, are you there?" asks Susannah.

I peer down the hall just as my mom's door clicks shut. "I'm not sure anymore."

Step Away from the Dinginess

At the far end of the playground at school, there's this bunch of little trees huddled around a ginormous flat rock. The PTA moms had it installed last year to show the middle-graders they know we're not babies anymore and that, instead of needing wavy purple slides and tic-tac-toe jungle gyms, we need private-ish places to talk about private-ish stuff. Susannah, Laurel, and I don't exactly own this spot, but since we probably spend more time there than any other kid at Allencroft Middle School, we thought we should give it a name.

Laurel first wanted to call it the Clubhouse, which made Susannah snort out loud, because a girl who'd soon be starring in actual TV shows and actual major motion pictures would never have a stupid clubhouse. But, if she got on a really big show like *The Garage Girls,* she might have a loft in Manhattan, which is a huge apartment with no walls between the rooms, big pipes snaked across the ceiling, and supertall windows overlooking the coolest city on Earth.

And, if I have anything to say about it, the place would have jars and jars of candy on the kitchen counter.

So anyway, that's how our big flat rock got its name, the Loft.

This particular recess we're entertaining. Sylvia has been here for about seven and a half minutes. Not that I'm counting. We're all sitting around here in our "lounge" area. I prefer to see clients on the lower part of the rock, the smooth area we like to think of as our dining room, but that part's all wet today. Could be from melted snow, could be from a dog. So we avoid it—just in case.

"So you're sure you're ready?" I ask. "Because we can go through it all a fifth time."

Sylvia nods. "I'm definitely ready."

Then Susannah, in an awesome and never-been-seen-before display of selflessness, asks, "Do you want to borrow my cape? I'd need it back as soon as you're done, of course, and you'd have to promise not to let any part of it drag on the ground or get anywhere near Smartin. But other than that, I'm okay with it."

Sylvia shakes her head no. "That's all right." She moves her hand closer to the black fabric. "But can I touch it?"

"Sure." Then Susannah, all of a sudden, yanks back the cape. "Are your hands clean?"

"Um, yeah. I think."

"Okay. Go ahead."

Sylvia fondles the material. "Is it cashmere?"

"Better," says Susannah. "Cashmina. Very rare."

Laurel snorts.

I look up to see Avery wandering along in the snow, all bent over like he's tracking a moose. And, like a gift from Lame Wizard heaven, Brandon is playing his game a few feet away with his friends. "Sylvia," I whisper. "There's never going to be a better time than right this very moment." I push her off the edge of the lounge. "Go!"

She stands up and dusts off her jeans. Then her hands fly up to her head. "Should I take off my hat?"

In unison, we all say, "No!"

"Right." She sucks in a big breath and squints over at Avery, who may or may not be sniffing moose droppings. "You're sure this will work?"

"Positive," I say. "Go get 'em, tiger."

We watch as she takes feeble little sparrow steps toward him. She doesn't travel in a straight line. **She weaves left a bit, then right, like a short kid desperately trying to catch a glimpse of the Santa Claus Parade from behind a wall of exceptionally tall and**

extraordinarily heartless grown-ups. Not that I'd know.

Then we grab on to one another because she trips over an abandoned snow fort and falls forward, almost, but not quite hurtling straight into Avery's arms. She loses her hat in the snow, but, at the last moment, she stays upright.

"Huh. She's more corrugated than you'd think," says Laurel.

"*Coordin*ated," I say. "Corrugated would mean she's all crinkled and rumpled."

We stare at Sylvia's cowlicks, which have formed horns on either side of her head. Susannah sighs. "Either word works, really."

Avery looks up at her and grunts a nongreeting, then Sylvia points out a possible moose track. I grin, shocked. Never once did I mention her joining him on his large mammal hunt. That was pure genius on Sylvia's part! (See, **this is a mark of a truly noble client.** After a while, **she absorbs your words through some kind of Unwritten Rule osmosis and begins to think for herself.** I'm so proud of her I could burst.)

Both bent over now, Sylvia and Avery start talking into each other's knees and, when Avery finally stands upright and looks her in the face, I see him smile. But what's more important than Avery smiling is Brandon frowning. He watches as Sylvia compliments Avery on his beastly ski jacket, which looks like it's made of silver oven mitts. Avery looks down and tries to shine it up—probably not a good idea if he's hunting moose, too much glare—then Sylvia executes an Unwritten-Rulebook-perfect yawn, combined with the well-timed glance around the playground. Just so he knows she's not stuck talking to him. She has other options, and may or may not be considering them at that very moment.

Then she waves her knobby fingers at him and, without glancing back to see if Brandon is watching, she pitches and weaves her way back toward the school.

My little bird is finally growing up.

$\mathcal{S}$o that's when I realized I left my science homework in my agent's Hummer," says Susannah as we wipe off the Loft and begin to make our way across the soccer field.

Laurel rolls her eyes. **"Do you think we'll ever have a conversation that doesn't have the words** *my* **agent in it?** Or *my agent's Hummer?*"

Just as Susannah's about to fling her cape around her shoulders and stomp away— probably to call her agent—none other than Devon Sweeney appears. She's wearing a quilted watermelon-colored ski jacket and black leggings tucked into fluffy black boots. Nothing she's wearing is made of cashmina, you can just tell. Still, and I'd never admit this to Susannah, Devon looks like she could be in an ad for a superfancy ski lodge. You know, sipping hot chocolate by the fire, surrounded by cute ski-instructor boys with windburned cheeks.

Susannah and Laurel mumble hello and I actually smile. I don't even have to force myself either. I haven't stopped reeling with happiness over Sylvia's performance and I might not stop for hours. When you're having a day this good, you can afford to be a bit generous, even if your Lama status is temporarily turned upside down.

Devon smiles, pushing her black velvet hairband farther back in her hair. "I hope you don't think I'm being creepy, but I overheard what you were saying." She's looking at Susannah. "You're really a model?"

"For now," Susannah sniffs. "I'll be an actress pretty soon."

"That's so cool. **A lot of people say I have**

beautiful feet. They tell me I should be a foot model. Do you think I need a special agent for foot modeling?"

"You don't want to get into parts modeling," says Susannah, shaking her head. "Your feet would have to be *perfect*."

I'm not sure I've ever met anyone who blushes as often as Devon. She laughs a honking little laugh and waggles her head. "And what if they are?"

"Trust me, they aren't," Susannah says. "One tiny mark can kill a parts model's career. So unless you've kept them wrapped in thick socks and tucked into down-filled slippers that could never cause so much as a blister for your whole life, it's not possible."

But Devon's already bent down, unlacing her boot. She waggles her head again. "Okay, I'll show you if you insist." **She whips off her boot, then sock, and holds up a foot so flawless, the clouds part and a single beam of sunlight shines down on it.** Somewhere in the playground, a harp starts to play. Okay, maybe not. But that's the kind of foot we're dealing with here.

Susannah drops to her knees in some kind of worship. "It's unbelievable. There's not a blister, not a scar of any kind. And the formation of your toes . . ." She looks up at Devon. "It's magnificent."

Devon shrugs. "I don't take special care of them. I just have supergood genes, I guess. Could you give me your agent's phone num—"

Susannah stiffens up in horror—**she'll give you her last Oreo, the answers to her math homework, and the exact size of her training bra, but she'll never, ever give you her agent's phone number.** Some things, she says, are sacred. But before actual snakes shoot out from between her teeth, Laurel grabs Devon's gloves.

"These are, like, the cutest blue gloves I've ever seen," she says. I'm pretty sure Laurel only likes them be-cause they're blue. They have feathery fringe around the wrists and each finger has rhinestones where the finger-nails would be. The kind of thing that might look fun on someone else, but if they belonged to you, you'd think they were the creepiest gloves ever.

"You like them? I'm so glad. My father designed them, actually." She supersmiles until I fear her face might burst. "He quit his attorney job to launch his own children's clothing company, just so he could dedicate his working hours to bettering the lives of me and my sister. So now he makes everything we wear. Whatever we dream up, he designs it and has it on our beds by the end of the week. My mother says he does it because he loves us more than *anything* else in the world."

I feel an invisible fist punch me in the stomach and I can hardly breathe. **Here before me is walking, talking proof of how my life was supposed to be.** I try to look away, think of something else—just like I do when the class has to paint lousy picture frames for Father's Day—but it doesn't work.

"That's so nice of him," gushes Laurel.

"I wish my dad cared enough about me to design my entire wardrobe," says Susannah. "On second thought, with his taste, I'd rather he didn't."

Everybody laughs, except me. "Wow," I say in a voice that sounds high-pitched and scary and sarcastic, even to me, "dedicating your life to crushed velvet and rhinestone trim. Now, *that* is fatherly love!"

They all stop smiling and my nastyish-sounding voice hangs in the middle of us like a big ugly burp. No one knows what to say.

Just then Janna Knudsen trots up wearing

 two different boots—a dark brown sheepskin boot on one foot, and a cream sheepskin boot on the other.

Looking at no one in particular, she says, "Haley's selling knockoff boots. Only nineteen dollars a pair. Which boot goes better with this outfit?"

I want to kiss her for interrupting us. I try to focus on her question, looking her over from mismatched boots straight on up to her dingy blond hair. She's wearing a dirty white ski jacket with faded jeans. It's a no-brainer.

I say, "Dark brown," at the exact same time Devon says, "Cream."

I look at Devon, shocked. Again, no one says a word.

The end-of-recess bell rings and kids scatter. Janna waves thank you and goes back to the small pile of boxes in front of Haley Reiser. Then Devon waves good-bye and disappears into the school.

"Can you believe that Devon?" I say to Laurel and Susannah. "Janna was totally asking *me*! Janna has been asking me for fashion tips since the year she wore her skirt backward during school assembly. Besides, the poor kid's dingy from head to toe; can you imagine how a pair of dirty-after-two-days, fake suede boots are going to look?

You might as well call her Dingy Girl. You have to train the eye *away* from all the dinginess, not add to it! **Just because her father designs fashion doesn't mean Devon is qualified to take over!** I'm going to have a talk with Janna right after—"

"Uh, Zoë?" says Laurel, nodding toward Janna. "I think it's too late."

My mouth drops open as I watch Janna counting out money and placing it into Haley's hand. Tucked under Janna's arm are the cream boots.

Rules Were Made to Be Spoken. Out Loud.

Friday morning I'm the first one in the classroom. We ran out of milk this morning, so my mom had to drive us to a coffee shop for hot chocolate and croissants to go. So not only did I get to eat breakfast in the car, I got chauffeured all the way to the front doors of the school like Susannah will be when she's in the movies.

I have to turn on the classroom lights because Mrs. Patinkin isn't even here yet. After I hang up my backpack and my coat, I blow Boris a kiss that I hope he'll remember when he's at Devon's house all weekend, then I head for my desk. Which I just now realize has something shiny and hot pink on it. And so does Laurel's. And Susannah's. And every other desk in the entire class, including Mrs. Patinkin's.

I scoot into my seat and pick it up. It's a fancy folder and it says, "Devon Says."

She wrote down her crappy advice and had it professionally bound? In pink?

I refuse to open it. In fact—I drop it on my desk—I refuse to even *touch* it.

Riley thunders into the room and tugs on my hair twice as he passes me. "Whoa," he says. I don't turn around because I can hear him picking up the . . . thing. "Devon wrote a book!"

I cross my arms across my chest, but don't turn around. I huff out a little puff of air. "It's not a *book,* it's a folder."

He whistles. "Still. Kind of fancy. It has all her rules in it." Then he pokes me in the back with the thing. "See? Someone beat you to it. I've been telling you for years to write down your rules." He makes a hissing noise with his tongue. "Now it's too late. It's *all* over."

I don't respond.

His head pokes over my shoulder. "Why so silent? You're not jealous of Devon Sweeney, are you?"

I toss my hair, which might not behave as well as Devon's, but definitely has more personality. "Not a chance."

He grins slyly and drops back into his seat. "I'm not sure that twitching eyelid of yours agrees."

Mrs. Patinkin is the last one in the classroom. She waves hello with her fingers, then picks up her copy of "Devon Says." First she looks at the cover, then she flips it open and thumbs through the crummy pages. "Well, well, well. We have a published author in our midst. Tell me, Miss Sweeney—would you be willing to sign my copy after class?"

Devon blushes—for a change—and nods. Then she holds up a sparkly pink pen that's hanging from her neck. "I brought my favorite gel pen. Just in case."

Ugh. Susannah, who hasn't touched her copy out of respect for me, leans close and says, "Don't worry. **No one who's anyone autographs in pink anymore. It's so grade school.**"

Then Mrs. Patinkin says, "Well, it's all very professionally done. It makes Devon's unique points of view very official, don't you think, class?" Then she turns around and writes *Official* and *Published Author* on the chalkboard. I don't have to turn around to see Devon beaming. Her smile is spreading through the air like tuberculosis.

I hiss to Susannah, "My rules are every bit as official as hers! I just chose the less traditional and more mysterious route of refusing to print mine. Writing them down makes them overly accessible." Which means people want to throw up from hearing them over and over.

Susannah lowers her glasses to show this is, in fact, one very serious conversation. "It is my personal belief that you have much more prestige by refusing to publish yours, and that you are, in fact, every publicist's dream."

I rub Susannah's shoulder. "You're good people, Barnes." Then I look over at Laurel to make sure she agrees and actually catch her peeking into Devon's book—I mean, folder! I smack my hand down on it and Laurel jumps back and shrugs as if to say she couldn't help herself.

My eyelid twitches even harder.

Mrs. Patinkin taps her ruler against her desk. "Zoë Monday Costello! I'll thank you to share your secret musings with the rest of the class."

Normally I don't mind when she does this. I just whip a superslippery compliment out of my sleeve, Patinkin practically weeps with appreciation, then she forgets all about whatever I got Zoë-Monday-Costello'd for in the first place. But today is different. My brain still hasn't stopped stomping its feet about pink folders. "I was just saying I've very recently discovered a new word that I hope to use in a sentence one day." I question-smile at Mrs. Patinkin. "With your permission, I'd like to try."

Mrs. Patinkin nearly levitates with excitement. She holds her stump of chalk up to the board so she can write down my word as fast as spit. "Go ahead, Zoë," she says with her breath.

I stand up. "The word I've discovered is *usurp*. It means to seize. Or to steal." I turn slightly to my left so I can see Devon out of the corner of my hair. "To dethrone or eject. And if one were to use it in a sentence, he—or she—might say, **'To help out is human, but to usurp is going to get your precious toes stomped on by very small, but very furious boots.'**" I sit and fold my hands on my desk. Mrs. Patinkin's face clouds over. She really wants to reward my effort but she can't figure out how. My bet is she'll fake it.

I'm right. "Yes. Good. Yes. Nice . . . sentence, Zoë." She writes *usurp* on the board and turns around to face us. "Well, ladies and gentlemen, you should all take Zoë's sentence as inspiration to reap the bounty of words that surround you. Now, everyone come over to the back carpet and sit cross-legged. I have a wonderful surprise for the entire class."

By the time the Fronties get to the carpet, most of the spots are taken except for a big empty circle around Smartin. With our noses begging us to sit *anywhere* else, Susannah and Laurel and I have no choice but to plop down beside him. We're mortally disgusted to see he's coloring his entire right arm and hand with blue highlighter. Even Laurel isn't impressed.

He nudges me with his inky arm. "Come on, Costello. Wanna hold hands?"

"You'd have to chop it off, sterilize it, and sew it onto someone else's body first."

"For you, I'll do it." He starts to lick the highlighter off his skin. Everyone falls over, groaning in toxic horror. Vile!

"Martin Seth Granitstein," says Mrs. Patinkin. "If you can refrain from swallowing your own tissue, I won't keep you in for recess. When you're outside in the field, under the playground monitor's care, I invite you to consume whatever you like. **In my class,** however, **I ask that you swear off human flesh."**

Martin shrugs—"Okay"—pops the lid off his highlighter, and bites off the felt tip. Blue drool oozes from the corner of his mouth as he swallows.

Mrs. Patinkin screeches, "Martin! To the office. And have the nurse examine you while you're there."

He stands up and points at me with a blue finger. "Can I have an escort? Sometimes I get lost."

I bury my head in my hands and squeeze my eyes shut. *Please say no! Please!*

"No!"

Once his sorry carcass is out of sight, Mrs. Patinkin closes her eyes for a moment, then smiles like she's never seen or smelled Smartin in her life. "I have very exciting news. The entire school is going to participate in a political-science experiment. **Each class will be developing an imaginary island and will be holding mock leadership elections.** Students in every class will be divided into two political parties, each with their own name and belief system. And each party will elect a leader."

Devon's hand shoots up. She doesn't wave, just holds it up with her fingers flagpole straight, pointed at the ceiling. When Patinkin nods, she chirps, "I hope to be a leader because my father always says me and my sister should strive to be number one in every endeavor."

I try not to groan out loud and Mrs. Patinkin says, "Hurry, Brianna. Go write *endeavor* on the board." She smiles at Devon. "That will be our final vocabulary word for the week."

Tall Paul puts up his hand. "Does that mean we don't have to speak in full sentences until Monday?"

Mrs. Patinkin closes her eyes, then opens them. "Absolutely not."

"My parents want me to be an orthopedic surgeon, so I don't have to be a leader," says Avery.

"You're never operating on me, Buckner," mutters Riley.

Avery looks around, trying to figure out who dissed his future surgical dexterity.

Kitty, a plumpish Sixer with purple braces, says, "My parents don't want me to have beliefs until I'm at least eighteen."

I jump off the carpet and hurry over to Mrs. Patinkin's desk. She's looking about five years older than when she arrived in the morning, so I bring her her coffee mug to remind her there *are* still things worth living for. Her mouth is too exhausted to smile, so she smiles at me with her eyes, then gulps the whole thing down.

"As I was saying, two leaders will be elected in each class, and will campaign for the presidency by making their political plans for the island public. This will prepare them for the schoolwide election, where they will make a speech in front of the entire school. Then students will vote for the leader of their class. Any questions?"

Mrs. Patinkin waits about three seconds for us to stop scratching and squirming, and start thinking up some crummy questions. Then she continues: "Good! Let's divide the class, shall we?" She looks around, then rests her eyes on the highlighter stain Smartin left on the carpet. "Everyone to the right of the blue line, shift to the right. Everyone to the left of the blue line, shift left. We'll add Martin to the group on the left. Look around at your groups, people. You'll be working very closely with these people over the next few weeks."

I look around me to find Susannah and Laurel made the cut—phew! So did Maisie, Avery, and a bunch of Sixers. And Smartin, if he survives. But, wait . . . someone's missing. I look around to see Riley on the other team, which totally stinks.

Mrs. Patinkin says, "You have five minutes to come up with a name for your island. I want you to be inventive.

Think of names you're certain have not been used for any other place on earth." She pushes back her sleeve and checks her watch. "Sta-art now!"

Everybody starts whispering. My group throws out gruesome words like Hizzletown, Junglasia, and Sonderland. **Then I come up with the most perfect name ever for a fake island—Zentopia.** Right away my group agrees on account of it sounding like the Zentopian people won't have to do a lot of work.

Pretty soon Mrs. Patinkin calls, "Ti-ime! Now I'd like each team to give me their name, and then we'll vote on a winner."

I stand up and say, "My peoples do solemnly believe our island should be called Zentopia." I do a cute little bow and sit down. My group claps and hugs me. I happen to know Patinkin will like our name because she does yoga every morning before school. I think she likes to find her own Zen state before facing a day at school with us.

Devon stands up and says, **"The island should be called Icklesius, which is a democratic combination of everyone's suggestions.** I feel it's important that each and every voice be heard—"

"We'll save our belief systems until next week," says Patinkin. "Zentopia and Icklesius. Both very unique and well thought out. Shall we vote?"

I stand up again. "Mrs. Patinkin. Since we're missing a member of our group, the voting won't be fair. It'll be fourteen against thirteen, since each person is obviously going to vote for their own group's name."

"Good point," she says. "We'll just have to use Devon's suggestion of combining both names. It's the most democratic thing to do. **We'll take the *topia* from Zentopia and the *Ick* from Icklesius and call our island Icktopia.**"

Which is the worst name an island could have.

As Mrs. Patinkin writes *Icktopia* on the chalkboard, I try to wave to Riley to let him know these teams stink and that the name Icktopia stinks even worse, but he's leaning in real close to Devon, who is whispering something in his ear.

Maybe the name Icktopia is going to fit this island after all.

Clear Your Head of Googly-Eyed Puppies

On Monday morning, I'm late for gym because my mom forgot to put my ALLENCROFT HAS SPIRIT! T-shirt in the dryer, and Mr. Garson won't let us take gym in our regular clothes in case we sweat all over them and he gets blamed for stinking up the halls with us later. So there I was at 7:30 in the morning, drying my stupid SPIRIT shirt in my apartment building's creepier-than-creepy laundry room, *wa-ay* down in the basement, where the spiders and the incinerator live. The laundry room is right next to the storage lockers, too, and the whole time my shirt was drying, it sounded like something in Mrs. Grungen's locker was whispering to me. So I had to leave before my shirt was fully dry and now I'm running to gym class in a clammy shirt.

I did, however, make time to pop into Mrs. Patinkin's empty classroom to make sure Devon brought Boris back safe and sound. There he was, sleeping in his food dish like an angel. Just as I blow him a kiss and turn to go, I spy a photograph leaning against his cage for all to see. It's a picture of Devon feeding Boris a bedtime bottle from an eyedropper. In her bed. And I'm not sure, but it looks like she's singing to him.

No wonder the poor pig is so exhausted. Her creepy attentions probably gave him night terrors.

I burst through the doors to the main-floor hallway and find Annika Pruitt standing in front of Justin Rosetti's locker, which is considered THE best locker in the school, right beside the snack machine and the pay phone that everyone except the teachers knows works without quarters.

I'm going to be totally late, but I cannot resist. I stop. "Annika, what's up?"

She beams. "Hi, Zoë," she sings. "How are you this morning?"

I ignore the question. It's Monday, it's not a holiday, and my shirt is probably growing mold. Besides, she really doesn't look like she cares. I point to the locker's open door. "What are you doing? Isn't your locker upstairs?"

"No." She bats her eyelashes, which are almost as long and thick and curly as her enormous hair. "**Justin popped the question over the weekend.**"

"What question?"

"He asked me to move in with him."

Whoa. I open the locker door a bit farther and, sure enough, there is Annika's flowered binder and beaded pencil case lined up beside Justin's fat, markered cardboard binder—the one he ripped the green vinyl from so he could graffiti it better. One wall is wallpapered with lovesick puppies and Annika's fringed hippie purse is hanging on a hook beside Justin's hoodie.

Okay. It's important that I handle this situation with tact. Annika can be overly sensitive, especially when it comes to Justin Rosetti. "Wow," I say, nodding. "I love what you've done with the place." I reach up to touch an orange tie-dyed scarf taped to the locker door. "This must be your idea. You've always had seriously impeccable taste."

She nods. "Yes. At first Justin was worried it might make the place too girlie, but I convinced him I needed to do something to balance all his manly energy."

I look at Justin's scratched-up Ozzy Osbourne stickers. "Good thinking. Listen, Annika, I know you've been against it in the past, and I didn't push it because you and Justin hadn't taken any serious steps toward this kind of permanence. But I wish you'd consulted me first. **You really should have signed a prenup.**"

She looks shocked. "A prenup? I don't want anything to come between me and Justin at a romantic time like this!"

"But it's exactly what you need. Without a signed document that lists who gets what when you break up—"

"Justin and I will never break up! We're going to get married one day and move to Australia, where we can live on the beach and I can make his dinner while he surfs! We don't need any prenup!"

This plan is flawed on so many levels, I can barely stand straight. But you have to take baby steps with Annika. "Actually, it's a little late for a prenup now. But I could do up a nice little postnup." I glance around the neighborhood and nod my approval. **"We're dealing with some prime real estate here.** Now that you've gone to all the trouble of moving in and redecorating, you might have some ownership rights. Certainly the longer you live together, the more you're entitled to. Are you really prepared to give up the locker without a fight, should something happen?"

"It won't. Justin and I love each other. Besides, Devon

Sweeney said prenups turn relationships sour. She's seen it happen."

This Devon is taking things too far. It's one thing advising people on sheepskin boot colors and guinea-pig care. But **now she's endangering people's housing rights!** "Annika, let's remember that Justin does have a history of being less than gentlemanly with you. Remember the incident last month involving the bottom of your soiled shoe and your soiled heart?"

With this, Annika bursts into tears. "Ooh, this is *so* confusing! Devon said as long as I anticipate his bad behavior, I can change it! That all I have to do is praise him lavishly when he gets it right and he'll turn out just fine."

I squint, tumbling Devon's words around and around in my head. Something's twisted up and wonky here, but I'm too clammy under the arms to tell what, exactly.

Amateur Orthodontia Is Not Permitted in the Cafeteria

Laurel, Sylvia, and I watch in horror as Smartin plops down onto the bench beside Susannah. On his lunch tray are four things: an apple, a squashed milk carton, a plastic fork, and a stapler. Susannah slides her lunch tray away from his and says, "There are rules at this table, Smartin. If you sit here, you obey them."

"Lay them on me, cover girl." He opens the stapler and shakes all the staples onto his tray, where they land in a puddle of milk.

"No licking of body parts, yours or anyone else's," Susannah says.

"Ouch, that hurts me where I work." He holds up his hand to Susannah. "High five."

She ignores his hand and continues. "No shoes on the table and no chewing of any table legs."

"I was kind of thinking *your* leg . . ."

"Ugh." She swats him off and inspects her shoulder for rubble.

"So anyway," says Sylvia as she bites into another dusty

rice cake, "right after I finished my homework, I asked my mother—" All of a sudden she starts coughing and reaches for her milk container, only it's empty.

"Are you okay?" I ask.

She nods and croaks, "I just need a—*cough, cough*—drink."

I grab my milk, then Laurel's. Both are empty. I start to reach for Susannah's but she sets her hand on it. "I'm sorry, but I can't. It's January and my skin needs the vitamin D."

Sylvia stands up and points toward the far end of the cafeteria table, where Brandon and the other LameWizards are shoveling chili into their mouths and shouting while they battle dragons or goblin commanders or jack-o'-lopes. She says with a gravelly voice, "Brandon usually shares his leftover milk with me."

After she leaves, we glance back at Smartin, who is cramming staples between his teeth. Every time he jams in another one, he looks up and gives us a big metal freak-show grin. "You never said anything about do-it-yourself retainers," he says with a lisp.

"Ugh," I say. Who would have thought I'd need a rule for this? **"Unwritten Rule #14. Amateur orthodontia is not permitted in the cafeteria."**

He looks at me and whispers, "Your *face* is not permitted in the cafeteria."

A lunch lady stops beside our table and looks around. "Who said that?"

Laurel, who never eats cafeteria food on account of the scarcity of blue-food options, is staring into the porthole of wickedness itself, Smartin's foul mouth. She crinkles her nose. "I think you have one stuck in your lip . . ."

Susannah stands up and climbs off of the bench. "I'm going to get another drink."

Just then Sylvia returns from LameWizardland, still sputtering. *Uh-oh.* There's a clientzilla look in her eyes that makes me grab my sandwich and start chewing. I've seen this look before in disgruntled clients. From my early Lama days, I've tried hard to keep looks like this to a minimum. I swallow, then offer a shaky smile. "Hey, Sylvia. Feeling better?"

The look goes from howling mad to boiling fury. Her nostrils flare into tiny sharp triangles. "No!" She coughs again. "And do you want to know why?"

I'm petrified to hear the answer. Like a brave little soldier, I ask, "Why?"

I can see now that her wings are trembling. "Because

Brandon said no. Actually, he said, 'No chance!' **Brandon has always shared his milk with me—every single time I choked on my mother's rice cakes.** And not just because he's lactose intolerant either. I could always sense there was something more between us. Something that goes way deeper than one percent with Omega Three Essential Oils. But not this time. This time he looked at me like he hoped I would just go away." She squints down at me. "Do you know what it feels like to be looked at like that—by someone you care about?"

I swallow. "Sort of."

"Your whole plan backfired! And now I'll never know where my love for him might have gone, what possibilities might have lain ahead for two innocent . . ."

Okay. I don't yet have a rule about this, but, even in my horror, I feel one brewing. It'll need some tweaking, but it'll have an awful lot to do with banning gingerbread-with-icing language that would make a unicorn want to hack off his own horn with a plastic spoon.

"Sylvia, everything is unfolding exactly as planned. First he gets hurt, then he brews for a while, then he thinks he should make a bigger effort with you. It's how Brandon operates. Believe me, it's the only way to get a guy like that into an airless auditorium to watch girls in tartan skirts kicking their overdeveloped calves to bagpipe music. You have to trust me."

She doesn't say anything at first. Just blinks. "I don't know. It doesn't feel right."

I pat her wing. "Believe in the system. Did I or did I not get Mr. Renzetti's wife to come back from the hunting cabin after he got those hair plugs?"

She thinks about this. "You did, I guess. The bell's going to ring soon. I better get in line for the water fountain."

"Atta girl," I call after her. I turn around and smile at Laurel. "She's going to be all right, that kid." I sigh. Laurel pats my hand in true #2 BFIS support.

"Uh-oh," says Smartin, chewing on an apple core.

"What?" we ask.

"I think I swallowed my braces."

The end-of-lunch bell rings, signaling us all to get out of the cafeteria and get outside or else we'll get detention. Smartin tears out, leaving the evidence of his Frankenstein dental surgery all over the table. I sweep the staples onto my tray and wipe up his puddle of milk.

Susannah rushes back into the cafeteria. She's out of breath by the time she reaches us. "Zoë. Red alert!"

"I thought we agreed to make all red alerts blue alerts," wails Laurel.

"What's wrong?" I ask.

"I just came back from the water fountain. Guess who was getting a drink?"

"Sylvia. She needed to clear her throat . . ."

Susannah shakes her head. "She was drinking all right. Devon was holding the water fountain on for her and she told Sylvia to take an 'extra long drink.' Even though there was a hu-uge lineup waiting."

I squeeze my mouth into an angry little ball.

"It gets worse. When Sylvia had nowhere to wipe her dripping mouth . . ." Susannah looks around before leaning in real close, "Devon offered up the pretty green scarf her *father* made."

We look at each other as the horribleness of the situation settles over us like really ugly, really moldy confetti.

Devon Sweeney is trying to poach my very best client!

Time to Panic

"Listen to this," says Laurel, stepping onto my elevator Monday after school. Her nose is deep inside a very shiny, very pink, lousy excuse for a rule book. "Grooming someone to be your Major Best Friend spells LOVE!" she reads. "*L* is for Learner. If you tell your MBF what you want from her, she'll be a quick Learner!"

"A quick learner?" I snort. I pound on the button for the eighth floor. Nothing happens.

Susannah peers over Laurel's shoulder. "*O* is for Open," she reads. "Open yourself up to your MBF's fears and concerns and you'll spend many happy years together. *V* is for Voice. Always speak to a new MBF in a calm, soothing voice so she learns she can trust you." In a calm, soothing voice, Susannah says to me, "Hit that stupid button harder or we'll miss *The Garage Girls*."

I blow on the heel of my hand—for luck—and hit it hard. Still nothing.

I have something of a love-hate thing going with elevators. On the one hand, with an elevator, I don't have to walk eight flights of stairs several times each day.

On the other hand, there's the creepy, panicky feeling I get when I'm stuck in small spaces and can't get out. I once Googled *scared of small places* and learned it's called claustrophobia and probably comes from a "traumatic childhood event." Well, I know exactly what childhood event caused it. It was when I was five and my gorilla-size and gorilla-shaped cousins, Liza and Lance, came to visit from Oregon. I stashed myself in Liza's pink suitcase during hide-and-seek and Lance found me and zipped the suitcase shut. He carried me around the apartment until his mother heard my muffled screams and made him open up. I fell out onto the floor.

Lance got half a day without video games. I got a lifetime fear of being packed.

"I shouldn't even be here," says Susannah, checking her watch. "My audition is in an hour and a half and I should probably go home and get ready."

Laurel looks up. "Is this for the fresh-face commercial? Just you, a bathroom mirror, and a sinkful of icy-cold water?"

"Yes. This is the job of a lifetime."

"I thought the TV show and major motion picture are going to be the jobs of a lifetime," Laurel says.

"This one's a stepping-stone!" Susannah snaps.

Just as I'm getting ready to whack the stuffing out of the button, I see my mother waving to me from the lobby.

"Zoë, honey! I need your help with some groceries," she sings before disappearing into the parking garage.

I look at Laurel and Susannah, who are looking at Susannah's watch and bugging their eyes. "We have to go upstairs or we'll miss the *entire* beginning," says Susannah.

"We'll do it all in one trip," I say, hurrying down the hall toward the garage stairwell. The girls don't move. "Come on!"

Susannah pokes her perfect nose in the air. "That doesn't sound like a calm, soothing MBF voice to me . . ."

"If we don't hurry, my mom will make us unpack the groceries, too!"

Laurel and Susannah chase after me.

Down in the garage, Mom is complaining to Mr. Kingsley that the garage door takes too long to open, so we grab the bags out of the trunk.

Halfway to the elevator—which still hasn't budged—we

start to run. Dropping onto the elevator floor, groaning from the cruelty of child labor, we pull the bags off our arms and Susannah and I lie back on them, exhausted.

Laurel goes for total button control. She hits all the top-floor buttons and drums her fists against the other knobs. The elevator isn't impressed with Laurel's sudden burst of energy. When she finally does her big solo finale on the "door close" button, the elevator walls shiver, then close, and the elevator car starts to climb up, up, up.

"That was brutal grocery-bag abuse," says Laurel, reaching for Devon's folder in her backpack. "We never found out what the *E* in LOVE stands for."

"I think I can live without knowing," I say, shifting my position so a bag of apples can act as my pillow. I close my eyes and pretend I'm on a sunny beach. "What about you, Susannah?"

"Totally. Put it away."

Laurel ignores us. "*E* is for Emotion," she reads. "Keep your emotions steady. Emotional highs and lows can be unnerving for your MBF. Nothing will enrich your life experience like a good MBF." She drops the book. **"Major Best Friend. It sounds so . . . G.I. Joe or something."**

"Being Devon's best friend probably isn't much different from being in the military," says Susannah. *"Drab."*

Just after we pass the third floor, the elevator jerks to a screechy stop. We look at one another. I crawl over to the control panel and whack the eight button. Nothing happens. I whack again, this time blowing on my fist first. Still, nothing.

My heart starts to pound.

"What's wrong?" says Susannah in a tinny voice. "Are we stuck? We can't be stuck! My agent and my mother are picking me up out front soon. In his Hummer."

Laurel rolls her eyes. *"Stupid* Hummer."

"Shut up, Laurel! You're just jealous!"

"Am not!" She reaches up to rub her throat as she swallows hard. Her voice changes. "But I am getting thirsty . . ."

"Everybody stop talking!" I shout. "I need to . . . to think. And breathe." I pull open the steel door to the emergency phone and peer inside. I decide that phoning for help is ridiculous, so I press the alarm button. It buzzes like a metal pipe full of mad beetles. I use the Morse code for SOS—three short buzzes, three long, three short—which means Save Our Souls.

"I don't believe it," says Susannah. "I'm going to miss

the audition. My entire career is over." Then Susannah does something unprecedented. She takes her sunglasses and hurls them against the back wall of the elevator. **It's such a shock to see her entire face, I can't speak right away.**

"We need to distract ourselves," says Laurel, pulling my mother's shea-butter lotion from a bag. She squirts some on her hand and rubs it all over her face like a mud mask. **"We'll pretend it's a day at the spa."** Laurel lies back like she's poolside and passes the lotion to Susannah. "I'm not sure if dehydration is blurring my vision, Susannah, but I think I'm seeing a . . ."

"What?" Susannah's hands fly up to her face. "I need a mirror. Someone get me a mirror!"

Laurel closes her eyes like she's getting a massage. "Maybe we can call your agent in his Hummer."

"This is no time for jokes!" Susannah screeches like a crazy lady. "Here!" she says, pulling out the aluminum foil and tearing into the box. She pulls a corner sheet from the roll and peers at her reflection. She gasps in horror, then looks at us with bugged-out eyes. "I don't believe it . . . it's my first pimple."

Laurel jumps up and knocks a few bags over onto the dirty floor.

"What are you doing?" I ask.

"I'm rationing," she says. "Splitting up the food into thirds. Everyone needs protein, grains and cereals, fruits and vegetables, and dairy." She stops. "Except . . ."

"What?" Susannah and I say together.

"We have absolutely no liquids. So even if we eat tiny amounts and huddle together for warmth, we'll be dead in two days. Three if we drink our own urine."

"That's disgusting!" says Susannah. "Anyway, I can't die. When they find my body, it'll be scarred by *acne!*"

"Nobody's dying!" I say. "Let's not panic. We haven't even tried the phone." Opening the tiny metal door again, I reach for the red phone and pick it up. Right away, I hear it ringing, then a miniature voice says, "Nine-one-one operator. Police, fire, or ambulance?"

Before I can explain that what we actually need is an elevator repairman, Laurel and Susannah grab the phone, both wailing at once—Susannah about her mother waiting in a black Hummer, and Laurel about dehydration setting in. By the time I grab the receiver, the line's dead. I hang up slowly.

"This," I say, "would be the

perfect time to panic." As I suck in a deep breath I can practically hear the sound of a pink suitcase being zipped up tight.

*T*he second the firefighters open the elevator doors, three things happen. Susannah scrambles over them like the stepping-stones to stardom they've become, I shoot under their legs and kiss the filthy ground they walk on, and Laurel returns to her poolside position and demands that someone massage her shoulders, all thoughts of dehydration forgotten.

In all the commotion, my mother's voice is the only thing I hear. She's lecturing Mr. Kingsley as she scoops up grocery bags. "Honestly, it's no longer safe to live in this building!"

"Safe?" I snort, guiding my mother toward the stairwell. "Where's the adventure in that?"

If You Must Cheat Death, Remember to Tell Your Boyfriend About It Later

I guess Mom figures almost getting swallowed whole by the elevator is enough torture for one day, so instead of forcing me to put away the groceries and set the table for dinner, she tells me to go take some much-needed "me" time in my room. Armed with a handful of chocolate chip cookies, I plop myself in front of my computer and send an instant message to Riley. (The Number One Unwritten Rule when it comes to cheating death-by-elevator-suffocation is to make sure to tell your boyfriend how lucky he is that you survived.)

zoelama: riley? u there?

riledup: zozyrgrrl!

zoelama: u know it

riledup: Bad timing z. g2g to class

zoelama: sumo wrestling?

o o o

Riley isn't your average guy. For as long as I've known him, he's disappeared every Monday, Wednesday, and Friday after school. When I asked if I could come and where he went, he always said no and to sumo wrestling class. Which I wasn't nearly dumb enough to fall for.

Then last month when I refused to go into the school dance because of my utterly humiliating fear of balloons, Riley tried to make me feel better by telling me something equally embarrassing about himself—that he was not, in fact, training to be a sumo wrestler. But that he was training to be a ballet dancer. Which I think is cuter than cute and braver than brave. Then he made me swear not to tell a single solitary soul.

To his adoring public—and mine—Riley Sinclair is knee-deep in ancient Japanese martial arts.

riledup: yep. lzl
zoelama: ?lzl?
riledup: later, zoe lama
zoelama: wait, did u hear wat happened to me today?

I wait for him to answer. I wait some more.
zoelama: ri?

o o o

He's gone. And not only is he gone, but he has no idea how close he came to losing me. And I have no idea how upset he would have been. Which means my perilous adventure was one big waste.

My IM jingles again.

g-ma: yo zo?

zoelama: hi g-ma, did mom tell u about wat happened to me?

g-ma: no time 4 that. Nursie'll be right back. I got caught.

zoelama: ?caught?

g-ma: cigars in the boys room w/ fritz

zoelama: i knew it! he's a bad influence on u

g-ma: o he's bad alright. heehee. They threatened 2 kck me up to 7th floor 4 total lockdown

zoelama: but then I'd have 2 take the elevator!

g-ma: 7th floor is ladies only ☹

zoelama: but they must know it's fritz's fault!

g-ma: they nvr saw him. and I'll nvr tell. don't tell ur mom, she'll make me stop seeing him

zoelama: u should stop seeing him!

g-ma: i've told u 2 much. delete this IM! Bye!

I don't know where this Fritz came from, but he must be stopped. He's turning g-ma into a teenager!

Rule by Humiliation. You Know, in the Name of World Peace.

This has never happened before. Ever. Today is the day we're meant to turn in our Icktopia drawings and mine isn't even close to being finished. Not only that, but there's a dried-up puddle of drool in the center of the island because I fell asleep all over my homework last night. Being trapped in a semi-airless metal box for an hour was more exhausting than you'd think.

In the classroom, Devon is sitting at Mrs. Patinkin's feet. It seems the hem of Mrs. Patinkin's pants has fallen and Devon is trying to fix it with masking tape. I whip out my mini-stapler and climb down onto the floor beside Devon. "It's better to staple a pant hem," I say.

"Zoë," says Mrs. Patinkin with a smile, "we've got this under control. Take your seat, please."

Take your seat, please?

I back away and slump down in my chair. After spreading my island drawing on my desk, I start to color in the surrounding water, pressing extra hard where I've penciled in waves and slowing down around the gang of seagulls who are waiting for the whale to blow fish out of his hole. My drawing might not be finished, and the dry riverbed might be slightly puckered from drool, but my version of Icktopia is perfect.

There are kittens, goldfish, and wiener dogs roaming free. Every beach has three trash cans that are emptied every hour and waiters stand on every street corner with silver trays full of chocolate chip cookies.

Right smack in the center of town is the Icktopian Jail—one tiny cell surrounded by bars. The only things in the room are a My Little Pony sleeping bag, a toilet with zero privacy, and a rack of my mother's ugliest dresses for prison uniforms. **I plan to keep the Icktopians in line using the threat of humiliation rather than force. If every country did this, I'm quite certain we'd have world peace.**

I poke Susannah in the ribs. "Hey. Did you get the Queen of the Perfects commercial?"

She lowers her glasses and looks around. "I got better than that."

Laurel scoots her chair closer.

Susannah's eyes light up. "I made it just in time, but only because my agent's Humm—" She looks at Laurel. "Because traffic was moving quickly. Anyway, the director took one look at me and called over a bunch of older ladies. They all just stood there, staring at me."

Laurel rolls her eyes. "Can we speed this up?"

"The director finally touches my chin and says, 'Look at this, she's perfect.'" She giggles. "And the old ladies agreed! So I asked if I got the part and they said, 'No, honey. We have something better.' The director gave me a card and asked me to come back in two weeks."

"Wow," I say.

Susannah beams.

"Ugh." Laurel slumps on her desk. "Why doesn't anything good ever happen to me?"

"Tell them we'd like our loft overlooking that really big New York toy store—FAO Schwarz!" I say.

Susannah slides her glasses back up her nose and sits back in her seat.

Not two minutes later, Brianna's head pops over my shoulder. She looks around, then whispers, "Zoë. We need to talk. Real bad."

"What—?"

She shushes me. "I've been thinking about this whole island game. You, me, and Maisie need to form an alliance." Maisie gives me a covert wave from across the room.

"What?"

Brianna continues. "These teams could merge into one at any moment. And then someone will get voted off the island! That's why we need to form our alliance. So we can stay strong. United so we'll make it to the final three!"

I don't even know where to start. "Brianna, there is no final three. We're voting on leaders, but no one's getting voted off the isla—"

Brianna hisses, "That's what they want you to believe!"

"Who?"

Brianna nods and crazy-smiles. "Exactly." Then she gives me what I guess is our secret alliance shake—she clacks her bony elbow against mine, which makes me yelp.

Mrs. Patinkin claps her hands and asks Devon to begin gathering up our island drawings. Devon walks up my row holding the pile of Icktopias against her chest. When she gets to my desk, she looks at my drawing and gives me an annoying little rosebud smile, then swooshes on past.

Twenty-eight Icktopias of all shapes and sizes stare down at us from the board. Avery's is so tiny he couldn't fit the name of the island across the top—only Icktop. Laurel's is done in every shade of blue known to mankind. Even the sun is bluish green. Susannah's island is surrounded by soft studio lighting, which she says is far more flattering than the cruel and unforgiving glare of natural sunlight.

"Okay, people," says Mrs. Patinkin. "I'd like each of you to stand up when I call your name, and apprise the class of your unique and individual vision." She looks down at her checklist. "Shall we begin with . . . Riley Sinclair?"

I personally think Riley is the perfect one to start with since he's wearing his hair all messy today. It looks extra-gorgeously cute. He stands up and looks at us through his bangs with a grin. "The magical lands I created—"

Mrs. Patinkin interrupts him. "From the front of the class, Riley. And position yourself adjacent to your drawing."

He stumbles toward the front and looks down at his un-laced shoes. I smile because I know he doesn't know what *adjacent* means. "Uh, Mrs. Patinkin?" he asks.

She lifts her eyebrows.

"Where should I stand so I can be extra-adjacent to my drawing?"

"Anywhere beside it will suffice."

He steps closer to it and begins. "The magical lands I created are unique and individual." The class snickers here and Riley fake-growls at them. "If you look over here on the right side, you'll see our mountain range. It's where snowboarders can catch some sweet moguls. I've added a terrain park with jumps, rails, boxes, and a wicked half-pipe and two quarter pipes." Some of the kids sit forward in their chairs and groan. Like they wish they were there. But only Small Paul really wishes it. The other kids just want to *look* like they wish it.

Riley points to another section of his island, which looks like his little sister colored it. "The waves on the west coast are always good for surfing."

"Are there sharks?" asks Harrison Huxtable.

"There won't be sharks after we feed *you* to them, Huxtable," says Smartin.

I smack my hand on my desk as a warning to Smartin. **What Harrison lacks in calorie control, he more than makes up for with impeccable personal hygiene. The kid's spotless.**

Smartin, on the other hand, wears his breakfast on his clothing and probably bathes himself in a dog dish. He's a walking microbe factory and has no business speaking to someone as speckless as Harrison.

"Thank you, Riley," says Mrs. Patinkin. "I hope you've left room for a hospital on your island. Or at least a fracture clinic with extended hours."

Riley grins and holds up his ankle, which he broke last year snowboarding. He fake-limps back to his desk. I wish I could fake-kiss him better.

"Zoë Costello," says Mrs. Patinkin as she squints at the board. "Am I seeing correctly? Is your drawing . . . incomplete?"

"Sort of. It was almost complete, but Laurel and Susannah and I got locked in an elevator and I had what some doctors might call a claustrophobic attack because of a childhood incident involving a rotten hiding place and a suitcase and a moron of a cousin, and by the time we got out of the elevator, I was not only starved nearly to death, but I was emotionally exhausted. I tried to complete my drawing but I guess all the excitement—"

Mrs. Patinkin interrupts me. Rather rudely, I think. "Laurel, Susannah—were you able to finish your art assignments?"

They both look at me, terrified. Like they're not sure if it's better to get reamed out by me or Mrs. Patinkin. I nod to them that they should tell the truth. Even if the truth takes me down. "Yes," they both say.

Mrs. Patinkin glares at me and scratches what looks like a big *X* in her book. "All right, then, we'll have to find someone with a less exciting social life to take the stage. Devon Sweeney, is your project complete?" asks Mrs. Patinkin.

"Yes!" Devon scurries to the front and stands beside a big piece of paper with nothing but a yellow circle on it. The circle has a silvery *Z* through the middle and is outlined in purple dots. As soon as she points to her crappy excuse for an island, the whole class oohs and aahs like she drew a geographically correct map of Hawaii. **"Icktopia means too much to me to draw silly little beaches and seagulls."**

Hey, I worked for two hours shading those wing feathers!

She continues: "The only way I could truly capture my feelings was to portray them with this symbol." Mrs.

Patinkin rushes to the board and writes *symbol* on her vocabulary list. Then she does something even worse. Mrs. Patinkin stands at the board with her crummy chalk, like she's certain Devon's going to be shooting off a whole list of chalkboard-worthy vocabulary words.

Devon says, "The color yellow represents warmth, the silver *Z* represents a dazzling future, and each purple dot represents a very special memory." She pauses to hug herself and rock side to side. "It was inspired by my father and all my hopes for him."

We all look at one another, confused.

"I mean *his* hopes for *me!*" she says quickly.

Then, just as I slump farther down in my seat and try to forget the pain in my stomach that seems to start every time Devon talks about her father, the whole class says, "Awww." Like she's talking about a lost puppy or a fuzzy caterpillar.

"I was planning to add a bit of sparkle to my symbol," Devon says, "to represent the spirit and courage of my people. Except my glue gun broke."

Then the worst thing possible happens. Sylvia takes a tiny breath and timidly puts up her hand. "Um, Devon? My mother has a brand-new glue gun. If you want to bring your island—I mean, symbol—over on the weekend, maybe we could add the sparkles together."

Mrs. Patinkin stands up and clasps her hands. "This is exactly what I was hoping for. This project is going to bring us closer together as a class." She looks at Sylvia, then Devon. **"Already I'm seeing the beginnings of some real Icktopia magic!"**

I have a word for the chalkboard. *Involuntary.* Which means I so didn't mean for anyone to hear the low-pitched growl that came scrabbling and churning up from the underbelly of my soul.

Sparkles Are for Good Witches of the North and LameWizard Lovers

The Great Glue Gun Meeting must be stopped. It's Friday night and I'm home alone in my bear-claw slippers and pajamas. My mom went out for pasta with her best friend, Jane, and promised to be back before ten, which means I have to work fast or else Devon's going to be welcomed into the bosom of Sylvia's mother's craft room. And one thing is certain—once Devon gets a look at the zillions of color-coded ribbons lined up like a rainbow in the Smye's present-wrapping closet, I'm a goner. There isn't a girl on earth who doesn't want to receive a gift wrapped in those ribbons.

Through a little detective work—I spied Sylvia writing her address on Devon's hand— I know exactly when the meeting is supposed to go down. Twelve-thirty tomorrow, just in time for Mrs. Smye's famous smoked-meat sandwiches.

I pick up the phone and dial Sylvia's number. There's a bonus to having known Sylvia as long as I have. I know her weakness. Chocolate. I pour a pile of chocolate chips onto my mother's bed and pop a bunch into my mouth. You know, for atmosphere.

Sylvia answers the phone. "Smye residence."

I sputter a bit on melted chocolate, then say, "Hi, Sylvia, it's Zoë."

"I can't really talk right now. It's almost ten and I'm sup-posed to be in bed because I have a big day tomorrow . . ."

I try to sweep the chocolate from my mouth with my tongue, but there's too much. "Mm, that's exactly what I was calling about. Tomorrow. I found a new chocolate shop. It's down by Bristol Street and they make chocolate-covered rice crackers. And I know how much you like rice crackers."

"Wow. Do they make them fresh?"

I sit up taller. "Yes! But only on Saturdays. Which is why I'm calling so late. Tomorrow's Saturday. I checked their Web site, they open at eleven. But I figure we should leave early so we can be the first ones there. That way we'll get the freshest—"

"Oh, I can't go tomorrow. Devon's coming over to finish her project. It's going to look really good once it's all sparkly."

It takes a second for me to reload my brain. And my mouth, which is watering for more chocolate. "I've always believed that less is more when it comes to sparkles. In fact, it should be a rule. **Rule #18: Sparkles are for Good Witches of the North and LameWizard lovers. Everyone else should just back away from the sparkle jar.**"

Sylvia says nothing. Little puffs of angry bird breath blow into the phone.

"Sylvia? Are you there?"

"*I'm* a LameWizard lover!"

I stop chewing. Crud! I forgot about Brandon! "Of course you are," I say, real quick. "Which is why you are allowed unlimited sparkle access! Much more than the average person! Haven't I always encouraged you to indulge your sparkle needs? I remember our class Halloween party, back in fourth grade, when you dressed as a princess and wore that shimmering tiara—"

"Zoë? I have to go now. See you at school."

Click.

My head drops into my hands. Stupid mistake! Insulting her taste in boys *and* her love affair with glitter. All these years, I've done everything I could to build up Sylvia's confidence. Like the time in kindergarten when she lost her first tooth. I helped her clean it up and polish it so the tooth fairy would be impressed by Sylvie's attention to dental hygiene. Then there was the time her brother parked his gum in her cowlicks and I had to work it out with Caesar-salad dressing before her mother saw it and cut her hair into bangs—THE dastardly enemy of the cowlick. She smelled like garlic for weeks, but it was better than walking around looking like she'd been electrocuted.

I grab the phone book from Mom's night table, then dial Devon's number. A man with a nice voice answers. "Hello?"

"Is Devon there, please?"

He laughs. "She might be." Then he just waits.

"Um, can I talk to her, please?"

"Su–ure."

"Can I talk to her today? Please?"

He laughs a cozy, Christmas-morning-by-the-fireplace kind of laugh. The kind where tinkly music is playing and outside it's snowing, but you're safe and warm inside. With your dad. "Well, I guess that can be arranged. Are you a friend of Devon's?"

No. "Yes."

In the background I can hear Devon giggling and saying, *"Daddy, stop it!"*

"Alrighty," he says. "Let's see if I can find her. Oh! Here she is, right under my armpit!"

There's more tickling and giggling and Devon saying "Daddy!" a few more times. I'm just about to hang up, because all this father-daughter stuff is making my throat burn, when Devon's voice comes on. "Hello?"

"Hi, Devon. It's Zoë."

"Hey. What's up?"

The plan was to invite her for chocolate-covered rice crackers. Or, if she wasn't into that, I was going to tell her I had top-secret news that she absolutely had to hear before noon on Saturday. In person. But the air went out of both those ideas. **Suddenly I'm too depressed to care much about the Great Glue Gun Meeting.** "Um . . . I was just wondering if you knew which questions we have to do for math homework."

"Sure, just a second. I'll go get it."

The phone clatters and I hear Devon's footsteps running off somewhere. Then I'm left with her father humming. It's a song I remember from when I was little. The Cruella De Vil song from *101 Dalmatians,* which used to be my favorite movie. I don't remember much about my dad, but it's possible that he might have watched it with me a few times before he . . . was gone.

Just then I hear the front door locks rattling, and my mother coming in. She drops her keys on the hall table and pops her head into her bedroom just as I hang up the phone and stuff it under a pillow. My mother has a few unwritten rules of her own. Like no phone calls after 9:30.

"Zoë, honey, are you okay?" She looks upset. "Did you hear what happened?"

"No."

"There was a break-in two doors down. In Mr. Mason's place."

"Seriously? Did he get murdered?" Mr. Mason always yelled at people who held the elevator door open for other people. It wouldn't surprise me if somebody offed him.

Mom gasps. "Murdered? Heavens, no! He wasn't home. But money was taken. So was his stereo."

"That crummy stereo?" I ask.

She sits on the bed and pulls me close. "That's not the point. The point is, it could have been our apartment. And you would have been here. Alone!"

"Good thing it wasn't," I say, my face mashed into her shoulder.

She lets me go and stomps into her bathroom, where she pulls off her earrings and starts washing her face. "This building has absolutely no security!" she says with a face full of bubbles. "That lock downstairs doesn't work at all anymore. Every lawbreaker in the city has access to us. Every thief, every drunk, every thug, every murderer—"

"Mr. Mason drives a fancy car. Plus he wears that fur hat. I bet that's why they broke into his place. Our car's a heap. We don't ever wear fur. We're totally safe, Mom!"

She spreads toothpaste on her toothbrush, then looks back at me. "I'm sorry, honey. I know you don't want to hear this, but it's time to call the Realtor."

Silence Is Genius

Monday morning. And there really isn't anything I despise more than Mondays. Unless you count balloons and usurpers. Not only did my mother spend the weekend looking through the paper for new, burglar-free places to live, but I have cold meat loaf in my lunch box and Devon accused me of hanging up on her on Friday night. Which I did, but only under the threat of an irate mother. Then Monday morning gets about ten times worse when I notice that Sylvia and Devon—by some fairy-dust coincidence—are both wearing red turtlenecks and jeans. The whole class keeps calling them twins.

I guess Devon's rule book doesn't have an entry about competing with your clients. While I don't like to brag about it, it's long been a belief of mine that a client is like a bride. **The client is meant to bask in the spotlight while I lurk behind the curtains and make them obey me.** Like a puppet master. Or Oprah's best friend.

Poor little Sylvia doesn't know it yet, but she doesn't have thick enough feathers to be sharing the glow of the spotlight with someone as attention-hungry as Devon.

And, just to make my Monday even crappier, **Laurel called me last night to say she saw Riley coming out of Devon's house on Sunday!** So, naturally, I dreamed about Riley and Devon all night. First I dreamed they shared a slice of chocolate cake and Devon started blushing because she got chocolate on her nose. Then Riley—because he's a cutie-face gentleman—smeared chocolate on his own nose so she wouldn't feel like a slob, and called her charming. And they went running around town with their chocolate noses and I didn't catch up with them until they got to the gazebo in Hunter's Park. Then I licked a chocolate chip from my pocket and smeared it on my nose so he could call me charming, too. But he didn't. He turned around, narrowed his eyes at me, all annoyed, and said, "Your face is a mess."

Today, in reality, he smiles at me as he walks into the classroom. He tugs my hair as he goes by. Which makes my insides go all chocolaty and warm. Until I realize something.

He usually tugs it twice.

Mrs. Patinkin raps her desk with a ruler. "Students, I

have in my hand what might appear to be twenty-eight squares of green paper." She takes a deep breath and shakes her head. "But they are *so* much more. These tiny squares represent the will of the Icktopian people. They are your voting ballots. Today is the day you'll choose two leaders—one from each team—and they'll campaign against each other to see which party will rule the island. Today you'll learn about real democracy." Then, without even remembering to write *democracy* on the board, she starts passing out the squares.

Up goes Stewie Buckenheimer's hand. "Mrs. Patinkin? Are we going to have a voting booth? Because Small Paul's already trying to cheat off me."

Small Paul moves away from Stewie. "I was not! I saw your retainer on the floor and I was watching to see if you'd step on it."

Stewie snatches it up and sticks it into his mouth. The whole class groans in disgust.

Harrison Huxtable, who is closest to Boris's cage, raises his hand. "I think something's wrong with Boris. He isn't scratching his neck today. And when I told him to squeak, he squeaked."

Brandon says, "I noticed that, too! His rash is all cleared up and he let me rub his belly."

"It's a guinea-pig miracle," says Laurel.

"Your *face* is a guinea-pig miracle," grunts Smartin with his finger up his nose.

"Who said that?" asks Mrs. Patinkin, looking around.

Avery and Alice snicker.

Devon shoots her hand into the air. "Mrs. Patinkin, **I've been giving Boris supplements and teaching him a few tricks so he can be the best Boris he can be.**" She blushes and explains, "He's never had a real master before."

He would have if *I'd* ever been allowed to take him home!

"We'll discuss Boris later, class," says Mrs. Patinkin as she turns out the lights. "There'll be no talking during the voting process. Your eyes will remain on your own ballot. And when you've written the name of your chosen leader, you're to fold your paper in half and put up your hand. I'll come around with a container to collect them. Then we'll announce our leaders."

Brianna puts up her hand. "Do they have to leave the island immediately?"

Mrs. Patinkin scrunches up her nose. "No one is leaving, Brianna. We're choosing our leaders."

"So we write down the names of the people we want to stay. Not the ones we want to vote off?"

Mrs. Patinkin drops into her chair and closes her eyes. She's probably wishing she'd become a yoga teacher right about now because then her students would be meditating. In silence.

Once all the ballots are collected and Smartin's is thrown out because he tried to swallow it first and it was too gooey to read, Mrs. Patinkin reads the names on the ballots out loud while Laurel and Avery tally up the votes on the chalkboard. Happily, my name comes up over and over. Unhappily, so does Devon's. Homer Simpson's name comes up a few times as well, which makes Mrs. Patinkin scowl. Once all the names have been read, Laurel and Avery add up the tally marks under the names. The final score is:

Devon, 12
Me, 11
Homer Simpson, 4.

Which means one thing. I better get busy.

Backyards Full of Trees Are Poltergeist Movies Waiting to Happen

It's Tuesday night. Just as I'm measuring myself on the ancient Little Mermaid growth chart I have taped to the inside of my closet door and never reveal to anyone, the oven timer buzzes. It sounds like prison guards are opening the doors to let a handcuffed convict out. Or lock her up. "Zoë honey," my mother calls from her bathroom, "will you get the short-bread cookies out of the oven? Lorraine will be here in a few minutes and I'm not finished with my hair."

As I'm hunting for the oven mitts, there's a knock on the door. I hurry up and let Lorraine the Realtor in so she can ruin my life.

"Hello, Zoë," she says, bending down low to look me in the eye. I hate when people do this. They try to get down to my level because they think I'll feel better about my shrimpiness. But I don't. **I just feel embarrassed**

that an adult has to fold herself in half to get a decent look at my face.

"Be a dear, will you, and take my jacket?" She hands me a heavy white coat, and when she turns away to check her lipsticked mouth in the mirror, I dump it on top of our winter boots in the closet.

Mom comes out from her bathroom and takes Lorraine into the living room, where they sit down and ask each other how they've been. Once they've both said they've been fine, Lorraine pulls a heap of papers out of her brief-case and sets them on her lap. Then she smiles at me. "Zoë, I'd like you to be a big part of this process. Would you like to tell me a few of your real-estate wishes?"

I think about this for a moment. "Umm, I'd like to live on a busy street. In a high-rise apartment. Close to a library. With a teensy, tinsy, slivery view of Hunter's Park from my window." I sit down cross-legged on the floor. "Oh, and we have to be on the eighth floor."

Lorraine's smile freezes on her face. "But, honey, that sounds like where you live right now."

"Exactly," I say.

"Zoë," warns my mother.

"It's okay, Jocelyn," says Lorraine. "I've brought with me what I like to call my Real Estate Needs Assessment. One for you"—she hands a form to my mom—"and a kiddie version for Zoë here." Then she changes her voice like she's talking to a stuffed giraffe, and says to me, "I think question-naires are fun, don't you?" Her lips curl all the way back into a smile that doesn't care what I think. "Let's begin. Would you like to have a backyard full of nice big trees?"

"I have a fear of backyard trees. They're too *Poltergeist*."

"What about a walk-in closet?"

"Too *Amityville Horror*."

"What about your very own bathroom with a separate shower?"

I shiver. "Too *Psycho*."

Lorraine puts the kiddie questionnaire back into her briefcase. "Maybe we should start with you, Jocelyn . . ."

"Actually," I say, pulling a paper out of my pocket, "I've put together a list of my own from Google. I like to call it my Real Estate *Costs* Assessment. The cost of hiring movers—$1,250. The cost of hooking up cable, phone, and Internet at the new place—$175. The cost of mail-ing change-of-address cards—$7. The cost of leaving loved ones"—I look up and bat my eyes at my mother—"priceless."

Mom laughs. "What loved ones? Mrs. Grungen?"

"We've had some lovely moments. Besides, she taught g-ma how to knit."

"Who?" Mom asks.

Oops. "Gram. I meant Grandma."

"There are certain costs that go along with moving," says Lorraine. "But the good news is that if you're buying a property, I don't charge you a penny. The people selling pay my full commission."

"That's okay, Lorraine," says Mom. "You don't have to explain. I cannot put a price on my daughter's safety. Costs or no costs, we're moving."

Suddenly a smell trickles through the air. It smells almost exactly like . . .

"The cookies are burning!" says my mom.

I jump up, scramble for the oven mitts, and pull out the smoking tray, letting it crash on the stovetop. The cookies are nothing but ashes.

Kind of like my life.

Storybook Cottages Belong in Storybooks

It's unusually warm for a Sunday in winter. Mom has the windows halfway down in the car and she hasn't noticed mine is open all the way. So is my jacket. That's the one good thing about being too small to sit in the front seat. Mom's way too busy driving to notice what goes on back here.

"You're going to love this place, Zoë. It's much closer to school. Closer to Laurel and Susannah's neighborhood, too. It might even be within walking distance of a certain donut shop famous for its Boston creams. The family who's selling it has to leave town quickly. Some sort of family emergency. So Lorraine says we can get a good price."

I don't say anything, just stick my head out the window a bit so I can feel the sickly sunshine on my face.

"It's the perfect house for us. You can keep your bike in the garage. No more elevators to get stuck in." The car turns onto a quiet street called Montrose Lane. One of the houses has a snowman out front and there's a tangly cobweb of tree branches over our heads. "See that?" says Mom. "These trees will be like a green roof over the street in the summertime. I've always wanted to live on a street like this. Just never dreamed we could afford it."

We pull into a driveway. In front of us is a brownish brick house with black window shutters and a matching black front door. There are pretty lanterns on either side of the entrance and a fancy mailbox sits on its own stand in the garden. Above the garage door, there's a black iron sign with a white center. The house number, 61, is painted on it in fancy writing. **The whole place looks like somewhere a character from an old book might live—historic, friendly, and well loved.**

It makes me want to throw up.

Mom's already out of the car and jogging toward the front door. "Come on, honey. The family isn't home, so Lorraine left us a key in the mailbox."

Inside, on the main floor, things get even worse. Every room is filled with sunshine, the family room has a big fireplace, the stair railing is perfect for sliding down, and there's a tree out back that would be great for climbing—if you like that sort of thing.

Upstairs, my mom takes me into the master bedroom, which has wooden floors and creamy-colored wallpaper with tiny flowers all over it. She spins around with her arms spread out wide. "Would you look at all this space? I'll be able to take your grandmother's bedroom set out of storage and finally use it."

I just give her a half smile and wander over to the window and look at the backyard.

"I've saved the best for last," she says, guiding me back into the hall. "Your room. It's got two dormer windows with curtains that blow in the wind. It's painted in crisp apple green with one wall in midnight navy. The floors are nice and creaky and under each window is a padded window seat that opens up into a terrific storage space. I bet the girl who lives here now keeps all her secret things in it. Come see . . . I think it's the perfect room for a young girl."

She pulls me into the room and turns around to watch my face.

It's the most perfect room I've ever seen. The roof is all slanted on one side and the perfect windows jut out in tiny peaks. The curtains are blowing in the wind. There's a trapdoor to the attic in the closet—which has special shelves and drawers for the girl's perfect clothes. I hate to admit it, but Mom was right. **It's the perfect room for a young girl. Just not this one.**

"Mom? Can we go home now?"

She wraps her arms around me. "I'd like to think we *are* home."

I pull away from her and run down the stairs.

$\mathcal{M}$om didn't speak the whole way back to the apartment. I could tell she was deep in thought, probably wondering whether she should hang our living-room curtains in the new house's living room or family room. At home, I hang up my jacket, kick off my boots, and go to my room, where I can be alone and get deep in my own thoughts, which no one seems to be interested in.

While I'm lying on my bed, staring at the wall and not making a short list of my Icktopian values like Mrs. Patinkin said I should, Mom comes and stands in the doorway. "Maybe you could get yourself a little rabbit. In the new house. You've always wanted a pet."

I shake my head. "Rabbits bite."

"Well, at the very least, you can babysit the class guinea pig. What's his name? Norris?"

"Boris. But the only weekend that isn't taken is next weekend, and we'll still be here. All the other ones are booked up by the Sixers."

"Tell your teacher you'd like to take him home next weekend then. The place will be a jumble of boxes anyway, what's one big, smelly cage?" Mom comes over and sits on the bed, which sinks down. I scoot closer to the wall so I don't fall into her. She pushes the hair off my face. "Sweetie, there comes a time when you have to move forward with your life. I know it hurts leaving the things we love behind, but you'll see—change can be a good thing. And you'll grow to love the new house every bit as much as you love this apartment."

My hand goes up to touch the horse mural on my wall. I've always called it *Horse.* Not too imaginative, I guess. My father painted it when I was small, back when he used to read me *Black Beauty* before I fell asleep each night. Mom says I was so in love with Beauty that I begged for a horse of my own. It had to be big and it had to be black. Then when my mom took me on a trip to visit my aunt's apartment in New York, **my dad stayed home and painted me my very own horse, complete with flowing mane, glossy black coat, and stamp-**

ing hooves. Mom swears I stayed up all night trying to climb the wall and ride it once we got home.

Now, in a small voice, I ask, "So you're buying the house for sure?"

"Yes, honey. I put in an offer yesterday." She squeezes my arm before standing up and walking to the door. "It's going to be great. You'll finally have a closet big enough for all your clothes."

I trace Horse's polished hoof with my finger. There's a splash of white my dad placed on the hoof that makes it look like her foot is shimmering in the light of the moon he painted above Horse's head. I've always thought if I rubbed it the right way—not too fast, not too slow—I'd be able to see Dad's reflection. The way Mom says he poked his tongue out when he painted. I move my finger across the gleaming highlight.

She's right. I'll have a very big closet. But I won't have this.

I ♡ Icktopia

"Be sure to remember to clean and disinfect his water bottle every day," Devon lectures me as I pack Boris's supplies into a small plastic bag. She follows me to my desk, where I grab a bigger plastic bag and stuff the food inside. "Zoë? Are you even listening to me?"

"I've been in charge of Boris since September, Devon. I think he'll survive the weekend."

She parks her hands on her hips. "See now, your attitude worries me. Survival isn't good enough. We want him to thrive."

"He'll thrive!"

She grabs the plastic bag from my hand and rearranges the food boxes. "Not if his yogurt treats get mixed up with his alfalfa!"

It takes every bit of strength I have not to cram alfalfa in her face.

It's almost 3:15 on Friday afternoon; and it's been a long week of slipping in glitter, which seems to be flaking off Devon's Icktopia campaign posters. My posters, on the other hand, are not about razzle-dazzle and glitz. My posters have heart. Literally. I came up with a great slogan for the Icktopian people:

Here's my theory. If you give people a mug, they can take a drink. But if you give people a *slogan* to print on a mug, they can sell that mug to tourists for ten dollars each and eventually make enough money to put their Icky little children through dental school so the kids don't have to spend their entire lives standing on a steaming-hot beach selling mugs to sunburned people in flowered shirts.

"And I like to change his shavings twice a day," says Devon, her voice rising to a hysterical yelp. "You know, so he doesn't get a complex about living like a, like a . . ."

I stop stuffing cedar shavings into my backpack and look up at her. "Like a pig?" I zip up my bag. "I have news for you. He *is* a pig."

"I find your attitude troubling. This poor animal is trapped in a cage and depends on us for everything. I need to be sure you're taking this seriously."

One thing I won't tolerate in my Icktopia—cages. **When I rule the island, the animals shall roam**

free. I watch as Smartin finishes copying the week's vocabulary words from the chalkboard, then walks closer and licks the board, leaving a big splotch of foul slime where *liaison* and *eminence* used to be. Then he belches.

Okay, maybe not all the animals will be free.

"If you see Boris fretting or pacing when you get him home, you'll need to up his carbs," she says. "My dad and I used to be joggers—"

"Why did you stop?" I ask.

"What?"

"You said you used to be joggers. Why did you stop?"

She widens her eyes. She doesn't move for a couple of seconds, then says, "We didn't stop. I meant to say *when* we jog; we double our intake of whole-grain pastas."

"Hmm. Well, Boris and I are definitely not jogging."

Devon follows me to the cupboard where we keep Boris's traveling blanket. "I just buffed his nails and checked him over for cuts, ticks, and lice, so you won't need to handle him too much. In fact, it might be best if you didn't handle him at all," she says. "And don't be alarmed if he swallows his own feces; this is a perfectly acceptable way for him to stock up on vitamins and proteins."

"Boris doesn't eat his own feces!" I say. "He happens to be very gentlemanly . . . for a pig."

"Boris is not a pig! He's a rodent." She looks up at Sylvia, whose arm is stuck in the sleeve of her jacket. "Sylvia, is Boris a rodent or a pig?"

Sylvia looks scared. She digs through her desk and pulls out a pink folder about half the size of Devon's rule book. The cover of this one reads, "Devon Says for Household Pets."

I don't believe it. Devon is trying to rule the animal kingdom as well.

Sylvia reads from the folder. "It says in the book—"

"Folder," I snap.

"It says in the folder that he's . . ." Sylvia looks up at me and apologizes with her eyes. "He's a rodent."

Devon enormo-smiles, takes the folder from Sylvia, and slaps it into my hands. "Keep it with you at all times," she says. "And in case of emergency, there's a list of after-hours clinics and vets in the index. You'll want the one that says '*small*-animal veterinarian.'"

I toss it back at her, but she misses and it crashes to the floor. "Thanks, but I don't need your project. Boris and I are going to do just fine."

"It's not a project, it's a book!"

I pull on my coat, pick up the bag of food. The bell rings and I start out the door. "We're going to have so much fun; Boris won't know what hit him. I don't plan to smother him with restrictions. I'm going to let him have the time of his life."

"Umm, Zoë?" says Devon.

I spin around. *What?*

"Aren't you forgetting something?" Her arms are folded across her chest and she nods toward the floor, where Boris's cage sits wrapped in the travel blanket. She looks back at everyone else, who are just getting up from their desks, and asks, "Am I the only one who feels Boris is in great danger this weekend?"

And the very worst thing happens. Worse than Devon cramming her lousy advice down my throat. Worse than my embarrassment at having forgotten Boris. **About half the kids in the class actually look worried for Boris's safety!**

I never would have forgotten him. Seriously. As soon as I got to the school parking lot, my mother would have asked me where he was and I would have run right back into the school. My mother's not stupid. She knows I wouldn't pack a guinea pig as big as Boris in my backpack.

Then Smartin tears over to the doorway and starts stomping his foot. He's blocking one nostril with his finger. Which is the universal signal for . . .

"SNOT ROCKET!" calls Avery.

And everyone counts down in time with Smartin's stamping foot. "Ten, nine, eight . . ." When they get to one, the whole class shouts, "Blastoff!" and Smartin splats one onto the floor by my feet.

Normally, I'd go inside out with disgust.

Normally, I'd make him disinfect the floor.

Normally, I'd smack him and recite **Unwritten Rule #21: Snot Rockets Don't Make You an Astronaut, So Keep Your Freakboy Missiles to Yourself.**

But today, I scoop up Boris's cage and smile at him. That was no random Snot Rocket. That was rarely seen evidence that Smartin Granitstein has a soul. I'm so touched by the way he came to my rescue; I bump him with my shoulder as I pass through the door. Honestly, if my arms weren't full, I might have considered leaning closer and kissing his chalky little cheek. "Thank you, Martin," I whisper, looking him in the eye. "There might just be hope for this big, bad world after all."

He snorts and walks away. "Your *face* is a big, bad world after all."

Okay, so maybe there isn't.

Paddling Pools Can Hold a Guinea Pig's Attention for Only So Long

Boris creeps across the bath mat and pauses to sniff the entrance of the Guinea Pig Fair. His little nose twitches and flares, and he makes a tiny squeak—in excitement, probably. I hand him the "Admit One" ticket I made, because I want to take a picture of him and show everyone all the fun he had at my house. Boris eats it. Kind of rude, but whatever.

Then he flattens his brownish-orangeish body down and scoots through the two washcloths I hung up in the entrance to keep out cockroaches.

He totally snuck in!

I got up super early this morning to build him his very own carnival. First I spread out a green towel for grass, then added the plants for trees. I gave him a lamp shade slide and filled our frying pan with water for a paddling pool. **You can bet your favorite underwear Devon never gave Boris a paddling pool!**

I thought he might get bored with sliding and paddling, so I made a fun house by smearing a mirror from the hall with hair gel so he'll look warped and crooked when he looks at himself. Then I found my mother's round baking pan and filled it with frozen peas to make a ball pit—just like they have at McDonald's Playland.

Boris heads straight for the ball pit, climbs in, and starts eating.

The phone rings. I grab it quick so it doesn't wake my mother. "Hello?"

"Zoë. It's Devon. I forgot to tell you something."

"I'm kind of busy right now, Devon . . ."

"You have to put the vitamin-C drops in his water. Otherwise he might get scurvy. And DIE."

Boris crawls into the paddling pool and splashes around. **And—I don't believe my ears—I think he's actually purring!**

"Did you hear me, Zoë?"

"He doesn't have scurvy."

"You don't know that. There are very specific symptoms. Is he lethargic?"

I watch him race in circles around the pool. "No."

"Is he hopping instead of walking?"

He hops into the center of the pool and starts drinking.

I flop down onto my back and stare up at the ceiling. "Devon, you seem like a nice kid, so I'm going to help you out. You're pushy. Pushy might cut it in a sixth-grade class, but you're in a six-seven split now. The stakes are higher, the kids are sharper. **You're going to have to take it down a notch or risk total social annihilation.** I haven't said anything to you yet, because I was hoping you'd find this out for yourself. But it's been over a month now and I feel it's my duty—my civic duty—to not only guide you, but—"

"Zoë? What's Boris doing now?"

I yawn, then glance over at the paddling pool. It's empty. So is the ball pit and the fun house. I sit up and peer inside the lamp shade. Empty.

"Zoë? Don't you dare hang up on me again!"

"He's, uh, here . . ." I look between the plants and behind the Barbie car monorail. Into the bathtub, the toilet and under the shower curtain. I check that the bathroom door is still shut. Then I notice one of the cupboard doors under the bathroom sink is cracked open. I peer inside the cabinet and see Kleenex boxes and knocked-over bottles of bubble bath. But no Boris.

Then I see it. Right where the pipes disappear into the wall, there's a big, gaping hole. My heart starts to pound like crazy.

After doing everything humanly possible to coax Boris out of the wall—laying out crackers, calling his name in my most sugary-sweet voice, and rattling the box of guinea-pig yogurt drops, I called an emergency meeting of the BFIS minds and snuck out of the apartment while my mother was getting ready to go get her hair done. Susannah and Laurel met me at the corner of Sycamore and Clark streets.

Laurel looks up at the Lisette's Lingerie sign blowing in the cold wind above our heads. "I knew it! **You guys are trying to trick me into bra shopping again. I told you the last time—my body will not be rushed!**"

"No one's bra shopping," I say.

"Then why are we standing in front of my favorite shop?" asks Susannah, staring at a pretty flowered bra in the window.

"We're not." I point across the street toward a small store with a puppy in the window. "We're standing across from Scranton Street Pets."

Susannah's mouth drops open. "You forgot Boris's food? Is he starving?"

"You lost his vitamin drops?" asks Laurel. "Does he have scurry?"

"Scurvy," scolds Susannah.

"Do you people have no confidence in me?" I say, determined not to cry in the middle of Scranton Street. "I would *never* lose Boris's food! Or forget his vitamins."

I wait for the traffic light to turn green, then rush across the street. "So then why am I not buying a tulip-covered bra this very minute?" asks Susannah, struggling to keep up.

I don't answer until we get to the pet store. Then I stop and turn around to face them. The wind churns snowflakes and bits of trash between us like a tornado as I suck in a deep breath. "I lost Boris."

If only I knew what's behind our bathroom wall, maybe I could relax," I say as we stare at the guinea-pig cages. I blink back tears. "I mean, what if he just dropped eight stories straight down to the cellar? He'd be dead for sure."

"It would be *nine* stories down to your cellar," says Laurel, snuggling a guinea pig way too white to pass for Boris.

Susannah elbows Laurel until she yelps.

"Or maybe the wall leads to the incinerator," I say. "It's

a big metal pit filled with fire. We do live awfully close to the garbage chute."

"Walls are filled with pipes and wires and wooden beams," says Susannah. "There's no way he fell into any cellars or incinerators."

Laurel shushes her. "I don't think we should be discussing this in front of the . . ." She nods toward the guinea pigs in her arms.

"What did your mother say?" asks Susannah.

"My mother got tired of waiting for me to come out of 'the bath' and left to get her hair colored."

"Huh." Laurel blew her hair out of her eyes. "Saved by foil highlights. What are the odds of that?"

I don't have the energy to consider the odds, so I continue: "He might have slid through an air vent and gone straight outside. He might be freezing to death this very minute while I shop for his replacement. Which would make me a murderer."

"You're not a murderer," says Susannah. "But Devon Sweeney would not agree. She'll use this tragedy to take you down."

"It's true," Laurel says. **"The kids would eat you alive. Boris is the only reason some of them come to school."**

A gurgling noise comes from my stomach, which reminds me that moments before Boris disappeared, he purred. Actually *purred*. "I think I'm going to be sick."

Susannah pats my hand. **"Everything's going to be okay. As long as Bogus Boris looks exactly the same as old Boris."**

"Don't call him *old* Boris!" I say. "That sounds like he's never coming back."

"He's never coming back, Zoë," Laurel says. "With all the rats and mice and bugs that must be living in the walls of that old building—why would he?"

"Hey! That's my home you're insulting," I snap.

Laurel shrugs. "I meant it as a compliment. Boris is probably having the time of his life. I think you're a hero. You set him free."

I sniff. "You think so?"

"Not really. But it would make a good Disney movie, don't you think?"

"Guys, over here," whispers Susannah from where she's squatting beside a huge cage. She turns around, smiling. There's a brownish-blackish-whitish guinea pig in her hands who could be Boris's once-attached Siamese twin. "I think we've found ourselves a pig."

Guinea Pigs Should NOT Smell Like Rabbits

I slip into the classroom as stealthily as I can while carrying a three-foot-long wire cage wrapped in a red blanket. After setting the cage in its usual corner, I look around before peeling off the cover, folding it up, and stuffing it in the closet. Luckily, today we have gym right after morning announcements, so everyone is busy looking for lost sneakers and SPIRIT T-shirts.

Bogus Boris is too busy chewing on a carrot to notice he now lives in the crummiest place imaginable—a school.

After I slipped Bogus Boris into old Boris's cage, I called my mother over to see how extra cute his toenails are—as a test. I figured if Mom scrunched her eyebrows and peered closer, I was doomed. On the other hand, if she took one look, scrunched up her nose, and asked when I was going to clean the cage, my plan was a success.

Thankfully, Mom's nose won. She didn't suspect a thing. She also didn't suspect that I slept on the bath mat Saturday and Sunday nights. Just in case. I woke up with a Band-Aid wrapper stuck to my forehead, but no Boris.

Here's my hope for today: that nobody notices me or Bogus Boris before Mrs. Patinkin comes in and asks about the "mesmerizing voyages" that were our weekends. Hopefully by then she'll have ruined every weekend memory we have and no one will think to welcome Bogus Boris back to the classroom.

Just after the late bell rings, Mrs. Patinkin sweeps into the room and throws her coat over her chair. "Good Monday, class! I can't wait to hear all about the exhilarating travels that made up your end-of-week."

"Mrs. Patinkin," says Kitty. "Does it still count as someone's end-of-week if they had to spend the whole time cleaning the basement?"

I could kiss Kitty. She's muddling up Mrs. Patinkin's thoughts before she gets a chance to check Bogus Boris's . . .

"Beverage container," says Mrs. Patinkin. "I see Boris's water is sparkling clean. To whom am I grateful this particular Monday morning?"

I pretend to organize the colored pencils inside my desk. But it doesn't make a difference. Half the class rushes over to Bogus Boris's cage to coo at him and ask him if he had a fascinating end-of-week.

Avery picks Bogus Boris up and kisses him on the chin. Then Avery scrubs his thick glasses with one finger and crinkles his nose. "Boris smells like rabbits. And he's acting like he's never met me."

But then Smartin—who probably destroyed his sense of smell two years ago when he folded a Christmas-tree-shaped air freshener and stuffed it up his nose—says, "He smells better than you look, Buckner."

Riley bends over and says, **"I think Boris looks awesome. Like he's been getting extra-special good care all of a sudden.** Little dude looks five years younger." He pretend-scratches his head and screws up his face. "I wonder who took home Boris-the-pig this weekend . . ."

"I don't know, Riley," says Susannah with a sly grin. "But he looks like the very best Boris he can be. I know I personally wish this person could care for him all the time. And I'll bet young Boris does, too."

"Boris doesn't look young! He looks the same age he was on Friday afternoon." Laurel winks way too obviously. "The *exact* same age!"

Susannah rolls her eyes. "I just meant that he looks like he had a spa weekend."

"Or a face-lift," adds Riley.

Mrs. Patinkin looks at the chalkboard and smiles. **"I think we have Miss Zoë Costello to thank for Boris's transformation. Zoë, do you have any special animal-husbandry tips you'd like to share** with the class?"

Before I can answer, Brianna calls out, "Animal husbandry is a crime in this country. So is first-cousin husbandry."

Mrs. Patinkin exhales and reaches for her coffee. "Animal husbandry means animal management, farming, Brianna." Then she looks at me, hoping I'll say something so she can pretend she's anything BUT a teacher. Even for a moment.

I say, "I've actually come up with a few unwritten rules for rodents. First would be that bathrooms—"

"Ouch!" says Avery, holding his hand. "Boris just bit me!"

Mrs. Patinkin hurries over to help Avery. "Oh dear! We're going to need a Band-Aid and some disinfect—"

Before she finishes speaking, I'm standing in front of them with a Band-Aid in one hand and a travel-size bottle of peroxide in the other. I look to my left. Devon is standing there with a glow-in-the-dark bandage and a tube of triple-strength Polysporin. I inch closer. Devon inches closer still.

"My Band-Aid is waterproof," I whisper out of the corner of my mouth.

"Mine has a nonstick pad!" she hisses.

It's like a very polite, antibacterial swordfight.

The whole class is silent. They all watch as Mrs. Patinkin looks from me to Devon and back again. She has no idea what to do.

*A*fter school, I burst through the front door and dump my backpack on the floor. Mom won't be home for another hour, which gives me just enough time to watch back-to-back *Garage Girls* episodes before anyone nags me about achieving multiplication perfection, or hands me a scrub brush and tells me the toilet bowl is calling my name.

I kick off my shoes and lose my balance, knocking a pile of mail off the hall table. I bend down to pick it up and spy a beige envelope from Shady Gardens Home for Seniors. It's stamped CONFIDENTIAL and URGENT.

Hmm. Right away I don't like it. If it were *only* marked confidential or *only* marked urgent, I could relax. Confidential might mean Grandma was running out of granny panties or face cream. Urgent might mean Mom forgot to include the check in her monthly payment. Again. But confidential *and* urgent has me worried.

I turn the envelope over and notice, like all mail that comes from the senior home, it's been taped shut. Which means two things:

> 1) Shady Gardens uses cheap envelopes that don't stick, and
> 2) It would be really, really, really easy for someone to pry it open, read whatever's inside, and tape the thing shut again.

I peel off the tape. Inside is a short letter.

Dear Mrs. Costello,

It has come to our attention that your mother-in-law, Jean Costello, snuck out of her room after curfew and exited the building. She was found waiting for her "special friend" inside the gazebo by the pond. We cannot know for certain, but we're suspicious that she was meeting with the very person she claims to have shared a cigar with in the men's room recently. We at Shady Gardens are concerned for Mrs. Costello's safety and would like to discuss with you the possibility of moving her to the seventh floor, where she would be under the watchful eye of Helga Triste, our director of security. If we can separate Jean from this friend, we are confident her behavior will return to normal.

Please contact me at your earliest convenience.

Sincerely,
Julia Wilkes
j.wilkes@shadygardens.com

I stuff the letter back inside the envelope. This is bad. I've met Helga Triste and her watchful eye, and I don't want my grandma living too close to either one. They're both mean.

Which means Mom can never see this letter. I race to Mom's room and open up her e-mail.

To: j.wilkes@shadygardens.com
From: jocelyncostello@webfirst.org
Subject: Jean Costello

Dear Ms. Wilkes,
I'm sorry to hear my mother-in-law is misbehaving, but I know all about her trip to the gazebo. You see, my daughter, Zoë, ran away from home that day and hid in the Shady Gardens gazebo. Being the dedicated and loving grandma that she is and has always been, Jean was arranging to send her granddaughter

home safe and sound. So as you can see, there will be no need to ship Jean up to the 7th floor.

Jocelyn Costello

Before I can change my mind about impersonating my mother, I hit send, which means two things:

1) Gram can stay on the main floor where the bird-watching is best, and
2) I'm officially a criminal.

"I'll Be the Sandbar Beneath Your Feet" Is Not a Song

When I think about the mood I'd like the Icktopian people to have, I realize it's the same feeling I have in Mr. Slobodian's drama class—I'm never worried about running out of glue, the air smells like sugar cookies with pink frosting, and I'm actually encouraged to experiment with making monkey sounds. If you raise people with that kind of freedom—especially in a darkish room with brick walls and giant red-carpeted steps that spiral down into a stage in the center—none of them will ever think about becoming a bank robber. Or a reality-TV host.

Because the big election is next week, Icktopian fever has invaded the classroom. Boys are wearing Hawaiian shirts and girls are wearing plastic flowers in their hair. Normally I'd be excited about speaking in front of the entire school, but with Devon invading my life more and more by the minute, I get a stomachache every time I think about my speech. Which doesn't even exist yet.

Icktopia is even on Mr. Renzetti's mind. He went to an educational conference and learned about something called Pervasive Learning. Which pretty much means cramming whatever we're studying into everything we do. So the cafeteria is offering "Island Fries" and "Beach Burgers." And today in drama we've been divided into pairs and are meant to come up with a two-minute skit that involves three things:

jealousy,
shark bones, and
sand in your shoe

The good news is Sylvia is my assigned partner. The bad news is Riley is Devon's partner. So as much as I'm trying to keep my focus on my number one client, it's not easy, because **Devon keeps showing Riley the hand-stitched sea horses on the toe socks her father probably knitted with his teeth.**

"And *this* pretty little sea horse is meant to be me," Devon says, giggling. Riley nods his head like he cares about pretty little sea horses and I try to catch his eye—to tell him he doesn't. He almost looks over at me, but Devon takes his chin in her hand and snaps his face back toward her other sock.

"Did you see that?" I say to Sylvia. "She's forcing him to look at her socks!"

"Wow," says Sylvia, straining to get a closer look. "Look at all those sea horses. I'm not sure, but I think one of them has a head that actually nods—"

"Sylvia," I snap, then smile sweet as seaweed. Sylvia looks so young today, the way her hair is pulled off her face by a headband. It actually does a decent job of paving her cowlicks. "It's easy to get your mind muddled up with visions of ocean life. All the pretty coral can almost make you forget that the ground beneath your feet has totally disappeared and your oxygen tank is almost empty. Then one big sixth-grade undercurrent blows in and suddenly you're swirling around in a flock of great white sharks."

Sylvia scratches her nose. "Flock?"

"And even if those sharks have black belts in karate and are selling fake books from the trunk of their mothers' cars, you're never going to be yourself until you feel that algae-covered sandbar under your feet. Do you know what I mean, Sylvia?"

"Kind of."

"Seriously?"

She nods. "You mean the ocean's a dangerous place."

Tears sting my eyes. I'm so happy I could burst. Five minutes alone with Sylvia was exactly what I needed to win back my number one client, my BCIS. Susannah looks at me from across the room and I give her a double thumbs-up. Which isn't so secret for, "It's a Lamapalooza!" Which is confusing for, "I'm going to take Devon down!"

But here's the thing about competition. It forces you to take a good look at how you do business. Basically, rethink everything. In other words, being a brilliant guide for Sylvia wasn't enough to keep her from looking at other . . . sources of advice; I need to step it up.

I need to hold a Client Appreciation night.

"We should probably plan our skit, don't you think?" asks Sylvia. "If I don't practice, I'll get nervous."

"We'll get to the skit. I'd like to tell you about a special event I have planned."

Her eyes widen. "What is it?"

"Not so fast, little grasshopper. First I'd like to tell you that I value my clients very much. And when you're a Zoë Lama client, well, let's just say, you're exceptional.

There are others who might try to woo you with flash and dazzle, but here at Zoë Lama and Associates . . ."

"Wait . . . you have associates now?"

I fake a surprised look. "Oh, didn't you get the memo? Yes. We've expanded."

"You mean Laurel and Susannah will be offering advice, too?"

"No!" I smile. "There's only one Zoë Lama. But they're acting as my assistants. They've been promoted."

"Promoted to what?"

"That's not important. What is important is that we're holding a Client Appreciation night and *you* are going to be our guest of honor."

She glances quickly at Devon, who is sitting on a step beside Riley and laughing at something he said. Something utterly cute, I'll bet, since everything that comes out of that boy's mouth is totally and completely ador—

"Who else is coming?" she asks.

I really don't like how close Devon's pinkie is to Riley's elbow. There's only one person in this room whose pinkie deserves that kind of elbow intimacy. "It will be your night," I mumble to Sylvia. "I only have eyes for you."

"What about all these new clients? The ones you had to expand for?"

"They're . . . busy."

Devon stands up and reaches for a straw hat from the pile of props. Pinkie disaster has passed. For now.

"Shouldn't we be planning our skit?" Sylvia says. "Mr. Slobodian only gave us ten minutes to practice. I really don't like being unprepared."

"We'll be serving double chocolate chip cookies . . ."

"I really shouldn't. Devon invited me over for something called MBF night."

I knew it! Devon is grooming Sylvia for her #1 MBF spot! Which totally violates *my* **Unwritten Rule #16: BFISs Must Be in Your Grade or Higher. Anything Else Is Called Babysitting.** This MBF night must not happen. "Okay, Sylvia. This was supposed to be a surprise, but there might be actual trophies involved."

She scrunches up her face and starts scratching like her nest is full of fleas. "Okay. Maybe for a little bit."

Yes!

Just then, Mr. Slobodian comes over and puts his hands on our unbelievably unprepared heads. "Time's up, everyone. Zoë and Sylvia, if you'd like to trot on down to center stage, we'll begin with your skit."

Sylvia peeps, "But we're not—"

"I gave you twelve minutes to prepare. On you go."

Sylvia glares at me and heads toward the stage. As she passes, Devon waves, then leans back on her elbows and crosses her legs. She swings her foot back and forth and something catches my eye. The heel of her sea-horse-coated toe sock is starting to unravel.

Frolicking Puppy Wallpaper Can Protect You from Exactly Nothing

Later that day Mrs. Patinkin is late coming back from lunch, which is never good. Smartin has his hand stuck deep inside the heat vent hoping to find things to snack on, Alice Marriott is drawing prancing kittens on the chalkboard and giving them names like Tea Bag and Spooner, and Stewie Buckenheimer has lost his retainer in the guinea-pig cage.

Tea Bag

Devon comes in with extra-rosy cheeks, and a few moments later, Riley follows. They both hang up their jackets and wander over to the cage—like their coming in late together isn't twisting one particularly tiny person inside out and back again.

Riley ruffles my hair and kneels down beside me. "What's going on? Has Boris learned to speak French?"

I want to laugh, but then I spy it. One long blond hair

hanging from Riley's muscley shoulder. I force a smile. "Where have you been?"

"Nowhere. I just went home for lunch. No biggie."

No biggie? I fake-smile wider and pluck her hair off his sweater. "What's this?"

He looks down. "Dog hair?"

"You don't have a dog."

He grins. "But I do have a goldfish."

"Must be some hairy goldfish," I say, turning toward the cage, where Stewie's hand is wrist-deep in soggy shavings. "And big. And ugly."

"Actually, she's kind of cute," he says.

I'm too shocked to blink. I can't believe this is happening. **Devon has stolen my MUCGIS! My Riley! And he doesn't mind one bit.** "Cute? Maybe. If you don't mind getting long blond hair all over your clothes."

"I don't mind a bit."

His words slap me in the face. In drama class last month, he and I were paired up and forced to do the trust test— where someone closes her eyes and has to fall backward and trust that a certain cute boy will catch her. So after Riley caught me, he made this big deal about getting three long, curly brown hairs on his rugby shirt—laughing and saying if baldness runs in my family, he needs to know now so he can plan his escape.

So the question is—why is Devon allowed to go bald all over him and I'm not?

"Whoa!" says Avery now, watching Stewie. "You just missed a hu-uge intestinal nugget."

"That wasn't an intestinal nugget, Buckner. It was a food pellet," says Stewie. "When are you going to get new glasses?"

"When your teeth stop growing sideways."

"Real funny. Want me to make *your* teeth grow sideways?"

Avery shoves him and Stewie hurls himself on top of Avery and starts punching. The class is chanting, "Fight, fight, fight," and Riley dives in the middle and pulls off Avery's glasses.

"You're the reason Boris turned cranky," says Avery, trying to pull Stewie's shirt over his head. "Your rotten fingers are always stinking up his cage!"

"Don't label Boris!" I snap. "It's bad for his self-image."

"Well, it's true. He never used to be cranky," says Avery.

Suddenly Brianna gasps. She's holding Bogus Boris belly-up and turns him around for us to see. Her face turns dark.

"Boris never used to be a girl before either."

Everyone leans closer for a good look. Except me. I step backward, and by the time I reach my desk, I realize I've made a serious mistake. I should have backed out into the hall.

Devon spins around first. She narrows her eyes and walks toward me. "You had him last weekend. And I happen to know he was a boy before that! Then you took him home. **Where is the real Boris, Zoë?**"

The room starts to spin.

Laurel and Susannah rush to my side. "Leave her alone," Susannah says. "She took way better care of him than any of you ever have. She built him a circus."

"It was more of a carnival," I say under my breath.

"She built him a carnival," Susannah repeats.

"Then what happened?" asks Devon.

"Yeah, what happened?" asks Avery. "Did he choke on a hot dog at the carnival? Did a roller coaster fall on him?"

Smartin asks quietly, "Did Boris die?"

The class goes silent as they wait for my answer.

"He had a little surgery," Susannah says, looking at me. "That's all. **The vet needed to do a small proce-**

dure to keep him mentally healthy. That's Boris all right. The *real* Boris. I know. I was with Zoë the whole weekend."

"You were not," says Brianna. "I saw you at the movies on Sunday afternoon. With your mother." A few people snicker.

"That wasn't me," snaps Susannah. "We hired a look-alike to throw off the paparazzi—"

I put a hand on her arm. "It's okay, Susannah. They should know the truth. Boris didn't choke or get crushed by a roller coaster. He didn't die." I pause to take my final breath. "Boris ran away."

Everyone gasps in horror.

"There was a hole in the wall and the phone rang and I looked away and he just . . ." Tears spill onto my cheeks. "I'm *so* sorry. You guys know I loved Boris. I feel horrible . . ."

"But not horrible enough to tell us the truth," says Devon. "You know, losing our beloved class pet is one thing. We might have been able to forgive that. But buying another and trying to pass *her* off as Boris . . . ?"

Riley steps closer to her and stares at me.

At this very moment, Mrs. Patinkin rushes in. "Sorry I'm late, people. Traffic was atrocious." She drops her bags and writes *atrocious* on the board. Then she looks around more carefully. "Did I miss anything?"

*B*y some miracle, Mrs. Patinkin sends me to the office a few minutes later with the attendance sheet. No one said a word to her about Boris not being Boris. Which doesn't make me happy in the slightest. Devon would adore ratting on me. The fact that she didn't can only mean one thing—she has even worse plans for me.

I take the absolute longest way back to class because I want to stretch out my life as much as possible. Just as I pass the darkened hallway by the woodshop, I spy Annika Pruitt wrestling with a dented locker door. Wood chips, balled-up lunch bags, and forgotten sweatshirts cover the floor and Annika is sniffling.

"Annika, what are you doing in this part of town?"

She looks up. Her face is wet with tears. "Justin told me she was his second cousin!"

"Who?"

"Tricia Hemmerling. He told me she was coming over

to help his mother choose carpeting for their laundry room."

"No one puts carpeting in their laundry—"

"I know that now!" she snaps, then starts to cry. "You were right. Justin was a total creep all along and I didn't want to see it." She kicks the locker and it finally bursts open with a loud squawk. Inside, Annika's books—carefully covered with pretty yellow paper—huddle together on the top shelf, which is falling down on one side. The whole inside of the locker is rusty and it smells bad. Real bad.

The girl is living in squalor. "So I guess the locker . . ."

"He kicked me out! He said it was *his* locker," she sobs. "I put my heart and soul into that place. I wallpapered!"

"Yeah. **Sadly, wallpapering doesn't get you any actual property rights.**"

"I should have listened to you. It's just that he's so manly . . . I lost my head."

Manly? The guy phones his mother every time he gets a C and says he'll hold his breath if she doesn't come into the school and make them change it. "Don't beat yourself up, Annika. It could have happened to anyone who's been taking advice from a Sixer—"

She gasps. "Devon chose the frolicking puppy wallpaper.

She dropped by with Cheese Nips. Believe me, Devon will be devastated when she hears what Justin did."

Frolicking puppy wallpaper and Cheese Nips—these are Devon's business moves? "The only thing I can suggest now is that we go after him for joint ownership. Which means you could maybe get the locker every other week. And alternating holidays."

"I couldn't do it. He's already talking about Tricia moving in." Her cheeks glow pink, which totally clashes with her orangey hair. "It would kill me to see her things scattered on my throw rug."

That's it. **Not only is Devon Sweeney going to destroy me and my future marriage, she's going to destroy the entire school.** She's taken her lousy advice too far. And these kids are gullible—they're willing to fall for the first swindler who pulls a folder full of printed pages out of their pocket. I care way too much about my friends at this school. I care way too much about Riley.

There's only one way I can beat her—and after losing Boris, it's not going to be easy. I have to come up with the very best advice the peoples of Allencroft Middle School have ever heard.

Bad Jokes Come Before Boston Creams

Other than my knee banging under the coffee table, the living room is completely silent. Outside, a bus roars along Chicoutimi Street.

I let out a big breath and smile. "This is nice." I look around the room at Laurel, Susannah, and Sylvia. "Isn't this nice?"

No one answers. I kick Laurel and Susannah under the table.

"Yeah!" says Susannah.

"Real nice," says Laurel, picking through the bowl of blue corn chips.

"Come on, Sylvia," I say. "Have another hot dog."

She shakes her head no and goes back to examining her cuticles. "I'm still pretty full from all the Tater Pops you made me eat."

"How about a pickle? Pickles aren't so filling."

"Nah. I'm allergic." Sylvia looks around. "So when does Client Appreciation night start?"

I smile. She has no idea the fun she's in for. "You're living it."

Before Sylvia arrived, Susannah, Laurel, and I brainstormed about how to make it look like we're an insanely fun bunch of girls. Laurel thought we should do makeovers, but we all agreed that Sylvia's "after" might not be any better than her "before." The only thing that's going to improve her head of snarls is a wig. Susannah said we should watch season one of *The Garage Girls* because she couldn't remember if Brie had bangs back then. So I had to invent a rule. Hair is not to be discussed in any way. And since people on TV tend to have perfect hair, no TV. And, since Laurel, Susannah, and I have kind of okay hair, no makeovers.

Which leaves us with really only two things: our sparkling personalities and a box of Boston cream donuts.

Sylvia looks at Susannah. "Susannah, did you go to your big audition? The one for the major-motion-picture role?"

Susannah hugs herself and nods. "They didn't even make me read lines. They just took a few pictures of me, oohed and aahed, and told me they'd call me back next week. My agent says it almost never happens this way and that I'm really lucky."

"How exciting," says Sylvia. "I've *always* wanted to be a model . . ."

Okay, this is very bad. If Sylvia starts setting her sights on impossible goals, it's going to be very bad for business. I need to change the subject. Not only that, but I need to start being insanely fun. "I have a joke!" I say. **"What's fuzzy and green, and if it fell out of a tree it would kill you?"**

Laurel throws up her hand. "I know! A poisonous caterpillar!"

I shake my head.

"A moldy blueberry," says Susannah as she brushes her hair.

"No," I say.

"A green kitten!" shouts Sylvia. "With supersharp claws."

Laurel falls over laughing. "Green kitten!"

"No," I say. *"A pool table."*

They all look at one another, scrunching up their faces. Then Laurel huffs. "Why would a pool table be hanging from a tree?"

"I never said it was hanging!" I say. "It's just sitting up there. Which is why the joke is so funny."

Susannah says, "It's not funny, Zo."

"Yes, it is." It needs to be funny. Insanely funny.

Laurel says, "The kitten's better." She starts to giggle. "He's, like, all fuzzy and green . . ."

Susannah snorts, "A green kitten would get *so* much TV work."

I clench my jaw and try to keep my voice calm. "Sylvia, what's funnier? Kitten or pool table?"

"Umm . . ." The room falls silent while she thinks. I can hear the clock ticking in the kitchen.

"What was that?" asks Sylvia suddenly, tilting her head toward the wall. "It sounded like scritch-scratching."

Laurel jumps up. "Maybe it's Boris!" She rushes over to the wall and starts banging. "Boris! Here, Boris!"

"It's not Boris," says Susannah. "The walls are filled with bugs."

Sylvia's face goes pale and I nudge Susannah. **Ugly rumors like this can sink a company. I smile. "Zoë Lama and Associates does not have bugs."**

"Boris!" Laurel shouts into the wall.

"Someone get a piece of cheese!" says Laurel. "We'll put it on the bathroom floor. As Boris bribery."

"Yeah! Only guinea pigs don't eat cheese. We need hay," says Sylvia.

"Where are we going to get hay?" asks Susannah, rolling her eyes. To me, she whispers, "Can I get the donuts now?"

"Yeah. But eat slowly. Otherwise we'll run out of things to talk about."

Susannah jumps up and heads toward the kitchen. She comes back with the box. "Boston creams for everyone," she sings.

"I *love* Boston creams," says Sylvia.

"Same here," says Laurel, pulling a spray bottle of blue food dye from her fanny pack. "I'm going to eat mine from the inside out."

"Me, too!" Sylvia says. "First I squirt out the cream, then I pull the hole open and separate the top from the bottom, then I—"

"Eat the top first!" Susannah squeals. "That's exactly what I do."

We all reach into the box at the same time. "Not too many, Sylvia," I say. "Remember what happened last time."

"What happened?" asks Laurel.

I explain. "Nothing. **Sylvia gets night terrors if she eats too much chocolate before bed. Screams like a sick cat in the middle of the**

night." I laugh. "Right, Sylvia?"

Sylvia goes pale. She drops her donut.

"What's wrong?" I ask. "Is it starting already?"

She reaches for her overnight bag and heads for the front hall.

"Sylvia!" I call. "Where are you going?"

A few seconds later, I hear the front door slam.

"Did she just leave?" asks Laurel with her mouth full.

I tear out of the apartment and find her punching the elevator button. "Sylvia, wait! Don't go, please!"

"My night terrors were a secret! You swore you'd never, ever tell anyone, remember? You said it right in front of my mother."

Ooh. I actually do remember something like that. Vaguely. "But that was a few years ago. I completely forgot! Anyway, it's only Laurel and Susannah. They won't think badly of you, believe me, if you knew half the weird stuff they do—"

"That's not the point. You promised you'd never say anything!"

"And I'm sure I meant it. I just forgot . . ."

She waves her hand toward the apartment. "I never

wanted a big event from you. I don't care about flash and dazzle. All I wanted was an apology. I lost my *boyfriend*."

I stare at her little face. "That's all it would have taken to keep you as a client? And friend?"

She nods.

I wrap my arms around her and hug her tight. "I'm so sorry, Sylvia."

She pulls away and steps onto the elevator. "Good-bye, Zoë." And, for the first time in years, the doors close right away.

Nothing Mops Up Brain Sweat
Like a Good Book

Sunday morning, Susannah and Laurel called to tell me to put on a tracksuit and sneakers and meet them at the public library. They said they had a plan to help me take down Devon, which is going to be harder than I'd originally thought. She got her hair streaked. I'd like to report that it looks perfectly awful, but the truth is, it looks awfully perfect.

The Icktopian election is this coming Friday and this I know for sure. **I will not lose to the dazzlingly highlighted Devon Sweeney, no matter how many golden hairs fall on Riley's shoulder.** We're meant to give our speeches before the Icktopian people vote, and Devon—who's been working on hers with her dad—has been spreading rumors that hers is *so* good she just might publish *it,* too.

What Devon doesn't know is that mine is going to be even better. As soon as I write it, that is.

I show up at the library to find Laurel and Susannah

seated around a table with a pile of
water bottles and energy bars in the
middle.

"What's this?" I ask, reaching for a
yogurt bar.

Susannah smacks it out of my hand with
the long stick attached to the newspaper. "*Not* until after
Round One."

"You're in training now," Laurel explains. "We've gath-
ered up every Dear Allie advice column from the last eight
months. We're going to ask you questions and you're going
to give us your very best advice."

"Then we'll compare it to Dear Allie's to see how you
measure up," says Susannah. "It's the only way to work your
advice muscles. Get your edge back."

"By the end of the day, you'll be in the best shape of
your Lama life," Laurel says. "Olympic level."

I raise both ends of the white towel hanging around my
neck. "So why did I need to bring this? Brain sweat?"

"Exactly," Susannah says.

I plunk my feet up onto the table, pull a bag of chocolate chip cookies out of my pocket, and cram two in my
mouth. "Okay. Let the games begin." I mumble through

the crumbs. Who am I to argue? **I don't know if I'm losing my edge or not, but I'm definitely losing my mind.** Sylvia has been declared Devon's #1 MBF, Mrs. Patinkin's class is barely speaking to me, and Riley is getting more hair-covered by the day.

And whether I like it or not, moving day is one week away. I'm ready to try anything.

"I'll go first," says Susannah, disappearing behind the newspaper. "Dear Allie." She pauses and peers over the top. "I mean, Zoë. My four-year-old granddaughter throws tantrums in the candy aisle of the supermarket, and when I tell her to keep her voice down, she hits me. What should I do? Signed, Battered in Boston." They both lean real close and stare at me.

I smile. "That's easy. **The kid obviously needs chocolate. Chocolate's filled with tryptophan— a chemical that makes people happy.** If Grandma makes her kid happy, she won't get whacked." I lean back and pop another cookie. "Next."

Susannah scrunches up her face. "That's not what Dear Allie said. She said that the child is acting up because she needs an hour of focused attention from Grandma each day."

"That'll work, too," I say.

Susannah and Laurel look at each other. "Okay, my turn," Laurel says, looking through the advice column. "I have been dating my boyfriend for two years. Is it appropriate for me to phone him sometimes, or should I continue to wait for him to call me? Signed, Too Much Silence in Syracuse."

I laugh. "You should wake up and smell the 1900s. And when you're done with that century, take a whiff of the new millennium. **Put lover-boy on speed dial—stat—and harass his carcass every time he's so much as sharing a subway car with another girl.**"

They're silent for a minute.

"Please tell me that's not what you do with Riley," says Susannah, shaking her head.

"No. I'm just saying she needs to be coaxed into civilized society. That's all."

Laurel bugs her eyes at Susannah.

"I totally saw that!" I say. The librarian shushes us.

"Zoë," says Susannah. "It's very possible you're going through a lull. It's nothing to be ashamed of."

Okay. This is my cue to take a break. I grab a water bottle and wander off into the aisles, running my fingers along the spines of the books and listening to the sound

it makes—like playing cards in the spokes of my bike tires.

This Lamarama training session isn't going to help. In fact, I really don't think anything is going to help me. **Could it be possible that Devon is actually the better Lama?** She does have youth on her side. Is it possible that rules look more official when they're written down?

Maybe it's over for me. I've had a good seven-, eight-year run. Most presidents don't last as long. Maybe I should be thankful for what I've had and move on. I could always take up knitting. Or maybe I could collect souvenir spoons, like old Mrs. Grungen down the hall. I glance at the bookshelves to find I'm in the animal section. Which gets my brain clicking and whirring. Didn't my mom say I could get a pet?

I bend down low and scan the books, crawling past the wild animals to the pet-care manuals. They have books for every kind of pet—from hedgehogs to potbellied pigs. Both of which would make my mom about as happy as the cockroaches.

No, what I need is something cuddly and friendly. Something that would help fill up space in that big old house. Something like . . . I stop and pull out a book about Airedales. That's exactly what I need. A puppy.

I sit on the floor and stare at one pouting puppy after another. They're so cute it makes me rethink my whole frolicking-puppy-wallpaper stance. Maybe being surrounded by puppies *is* a solid way to build a relationship.

I reach for another book—this one's on dog care. It's a pretty good one, too. The puppies don't look quite as big-eyed, but there's lots of good information on things like how to teach your puppy to go down the stairs and how to keep him from eating out of the cat's litter box. I look around to make sure no one's looking before folding down the corner of that page. I might need the litter-box advice for Smartin one day.

Or maybe Devon will.

I sip from my water bottle and turn to a page about training. There's this special program they use called LOVE. Hmm. *L* is for Learner—if you tell your new pal what you want, she'll be a quick learner. *O* is for Open—open yourself up to your MBF's fears and concerns and you'll spend many happy years together.

V is for Voice. Always speak to a new MBF in a calm,

soothing voice so she learns she can trust you. A calm, soothing voice . . .

I choke on my water.

This is *Devon's* advice!

I tear back to the table, where Susannah and Laurel are taking some kind of coaches' break and scarfing down all the energy bars. I slap the book down on the messy table, ignoring the shushing that is coming from every which direction. "How much do you dudes love me?"

Susannah snorts, "I'll love you a whole lot more when you get that book off my new purse."

"This training session is over," I say.

"I hate to tell you, Zoë, but it's barely begun. In case you hadn't noticed, Round One completely blew. I've been thinking for our next round—"

"There'll be no next round. Turns out that hooking your arm through your boyfriend's and saying 'Let's go,' then praising him lavishly isn't actually the best way to get your boyfriend to go shampoo shopping with you; it's how to avoid hesitation in your pet beagle! And putting meat tenderizer on Harrison's submarine sandwich is not going to get him to lose weight, it's how to get a pup to stop eating his own poop!"

Laurel and Susannah's eyes bug out so far they just might drop out onto the table.

"That's right," I say. **"Devon's advice comes from a dog-care manual. Every last bit of it!"**

"Shut up!" says Susannah, grabbing the book from my hand.

"That's not the best part. Flip to page 137."

Susannah flips forward and starts reading. Then she stops and looks up at me slowly. "No . . ."

"Yes." I turn the book around for Laurel to see. "*MBF* doesn't stand for Major Best Friend at all. It stands for *Man's Best Friend!*"

Laurel shrieks and grabs for the book. She scans the page. "Do you realize what you've just done, O Zoë Lama? You've not only won the Icktopia election, you've won your place back as rightful ruler of the whole school."

A slow smile stretches across my face.

Life Swapping Not Recommended

"Zoë," my mother calls from the living room later Sunday afternoon. "How's it going in there? I hope you're busy packing up your closet. The moving truck arrives next Saturday whether you're ready or not."

I'm lying on my bed writing my election speech, which will start out something like this: *What do choke chains, liver snaps, and student ID cards have in common? Everything if you're a student at Allencroft Middle School—where you're all being treated like DOGS!* I can already hear the whole school gasp. Especially Riley.

"Can't hear you, Mom. I'm too busy packing up my closet," I say. For effect, I crinkle a few sheets of paper.

"That's wonderful, honey. I'm glad to see you're coming around to the whole moving thing. Lorraine tells me there's a girl your age living right next door. I'll bet she smells way better than Mrs. Grungen."

"I bet she doesn't."

The doorbell rings.

"Honey, will you get that, I'm busy—"

I roll off my bed. "I know, I know. You're busy packing." I open the front door to see none other than Lorraine the home wrecker. "Oh, hi."

She shoots me a full-of-herself smile and breezes right past in a cloud of perfume that smells so horrendous it could probably clear the whole building of cockroaches. If cockroaches have noses, that is. And if they don't, today they're the lucky ones.

"Mo-om, it's Lorrai-aine," I call, but I should have saved my breath. Lorraine's already following the sound of packing tape into the living room.

Lorraine flaps a handful of papers in front of Mom. "Guess what I've got for my very best client . . ."

"Our keys!" Mom jumps up and snatches them. She waves them in the air and smiles at me. "Look, Zoë. The signing papers for our very first home! Isn't this exciting?"

"Hugely," I say.

"*Zoë,*" she warns.

I spin and head back to my room.

"I'm sorry, Lorraine," says Mom. "She's been so upbeat all weekend, I thought . . ."

Lorraine says, "Don't drag yourself down. This is a real milestone for you, and you should enjoy it. Believe me, I've seen more than one moving day dampened by the careless remark of a quarrelsome child."

I mutter, **"Your *face* is the careless remark of a quarrelsome child."**

Lorraine looks around. "Did somebody say something?"

I disappear into my room, dive onto my bed, and pick up my speech.

Mom and the Evil One are talking so loud, I can hardly concentrate on destroying Devon. I get up again to close the door, and just before it clicks shut, I hear Lorraine say, "The Sweeneys were motivated to sell to you because they're leaving the city . . ."

The Sweeneys?

Lorraine continues: "They have two little girls—Devon and Charlie, both beautifully behaved—and two golden retrievers. Terrible story. They're staying with family for a couple of weeks before the father begins treatment in Boston. Without it, doctors don't think he'll live to see next Christmas. And even with it . . . well, let's just say it's iffy."

Devon's father is dying?

I cross the room and drop down onto my bed again. The weirdest things are swirling through my head—like the way Devon's unraveling sea-horse socks matched her ponytail holder. And the way she described her Icktopia drawing—"It was inspired by my father and all my hopes for him."

It's Devon's house I'm moving into. Maybe even her bedroom. Lorraine's words ring in my head. "Without this treatment, doctors don't think he'll live to see next Christmas." I pull my knees in close and hug myself. I don't know much about what it's like to be Devon Sweeney, but I do know this much: I've never once stopped missing *my* dad.

This is starting to feel creepy. Like I'm moving into her life and she's moving into mine.

You Gotta Know When to Fold 'Em

It's Friday. Election day. Every kid and every teacher are jam-packed into the auditorium to watch each class pick a leader. Then, once the leaders are elected, their names get engraved on a special plaque that will be hung outside of Mr. Renzetti's office for evermore. I think it'll be like having a permanent Get-Out-of-Jail-Free card, because you can't exactly punish someone who's the leader of their very own island.

Lolly Rosen and Katie Carney are on-stage now. They're second-graders and to hear them talk about how they'd run their island is pretty funny. Lolly says the trees would be made of Tootsie Pops and the sun would never set because she's afraid of the dark. Katie doesn't give a darn about the sun; she just wants the whole place to be crawling with puppies so she can tickle them all day.

Susannah smirks. "I can recommend the perfect book for Katie's island's library. So she can make sure they all become her *MBFs*."

Laurel pulls the dog book out from under her blue hoodie. "Man's Best Friend. This crowd is going to go crazy when Zoë cracks the news."

Susannah and I look at each other. "It's *break* the news. You can't crack news," I say.

Laurel bugs her eyes. "You can when the news is *this* big."

"Are you ready, Zoë?" whispers Susannah. "Do you want me to look over your speech before you go up?"

"Nah. I'm good." What I'm about to do will surprise even Susannah and Laurel.

The whole auditorium is dark except for the stage, which is lit by spotlights—one over each podium. Behind the podiums, the red velvet curtain is pulled open all the way to show off each grade's sign. Our gigantic Icktopia banner is way over to the right, where you can hardly see it. Which is good, since if you look real close you can see a yellowish smear in the shape of Smartin's body—from when he tried to lie down on the sunniest spot on the beach.

We're sitting in the front row—Laurel and Susannah got here real early so they could watch Devon's reaction up close and personal. Both are sitting up tall, nearly shaking with excitement as they wait for Paula McAdams in sixth grade to finish her speech so I can take Devon down and restore world balance at school. **Laurel says ever since I got quarantined with chicken pox, it's been like the earth started spinning in the wrong direction like it does in Australia.** Susannah and I didn't have nearly enough energy to explain that one.

Finally, Mrs. Patinkin steps up onto the stage. "Thank you, Paula. And now it's time for the candidates from my class to take the stage. Please give a warm welcome to Devon Sweeney and Zoë Monday Costellooo." Then, because she's starting to enjoy speaking into the microphone, she says again, "Devon Sweeney and Zoë Monday Costellooo."

A few people giggle about the Monday thing. I make a mental note who, so I can remember to snub them later.

"Don't worry that she announced Devon first, Zoë," whispers Laurel as I stand up. "You're almost always first with us." Susannah elbows her hard.

Up onstage, the lights are hot and it's hard to see anyone in the audience through the squinty glare. Mrs. Patinkin sends me over to the far podium and sets Devon up at the other. While Mr. Renzetti threatens to lock up anyone who keeps talking, I look over at Devon. She's wearing a soft pink suit with intricate pink embroidery on the cuffs of the sleeves and up one side of the skirt. It's beautiful. Her father made it, although she admitted this morning that it's been a while since he's made her anything new. Even I have to admit, she looks every bit the leader of our little island.

Mrs. Patinkin isn't ready to give up the microphone just yet. "My class has named their island Icktopia." The whole crowd busts up laughing and someone throws a balled-up paper onto the stage. "Now, now. Simmer down, people. These two young ladies have worked hard—"

Mr. Renzetti clears his throat and points at his watch.

"Oh yes!" says Mrs. Patinkin. "Devon, you may start . . ."

Devon squints into the lights and tilts her microphone up higher so she doesn't have to stoop. "My name is Devon Sweeney. I plan to create a society of people who know how to work for what they want, but aren't afraid to take a little time off to enjoy it. My Icktopia will be one of environmental respect. Where humans and nature exist in harmony, not at each other's expense. We'll have solar-powered buildings, and we'll work extra hard to make sure the beautiful waters surrounding our island don't get polluted. A portion of every person's paycheck will go toward making sure no one goes hungry, no one is homeless, no one goes without medical care. **My Icktopia will have the very best hospital in the world. It'll be a place that can cure all people."**

She stops here and slips her cue cards into her pocket. "My father always tells me I can do anything I want in this world. He told me that people who succeed aren't smarter, stronger, or more special. He told me that I have all the tools I need to achieve my dreams and that all I need to do is work harder and want it more than anyone else." She smiles, but under the spotlight her smile looks more like a frown. "I want to win this election more than anyone else. I want to win it for my father. Thank you."

Everyone in the audience claps like crazy and Mrs. Patinkin dabs her eyes with Kleenex. Laurel and Susannah start chanting, "Zoë, Zoë, Zoë . . ." The plan was for me to announce my vision for Icktopia, quickly veering off into how great we'd treat all the dogs, then expose how Devon would treat the *people* like dogs. At that point, Laurel would slide the dog training book onto the stage so I could hold it up for all to see. This would make Devon confess and cry all over her clothing, then take off because the kids of Allencroft would run her out of town.

The room goes silent and I tilt the microphone down lower so I don't have to stand on my tippy toes. "My vision of Icktopia is all about people. Because without family and friends, all the pollution control and respect for nature in the world won't make for much happiness. My Icktopia is about sisters and brothers, mothers and fathers." I look at Devon quickly. "What I want more than anything else is for Icktopia to have a leader who lives that vision every single day. In what she wears to school, in the inspiration for her artwork, in the effort she puts into everything she does."

Kids are starting to mumble and shift around.

"So if you agree with my vision for Icktopia, you'll do like I'm going to do and vote for the best leader possible." I place my ballot on the podium and make a big black *X* in one box. Then I fold my vote in half and look at the audience. "You'll vote for Devon Sweeney."

Sometimes a Cigar Is Just a Cigar

I burst through the front door Friday after school and stop dead in my tracks. Mom is leaning against the hall table with her arms folded across her chest. She's wearing a coat, boots, and a major frown.

"I just got a call from Shady Gardens," she says as I toss my backpack into the corner and start to tug off my jacket. "Keep your coat on, miss. You can tell me all about a certain mystery e-mail on the way to your grandmother's nursing home."

Uh-oh. It's going to be a long drive.

As soon as we get to Shady Gardens, Mom points me in the direction of Gram's room and hurries off to discuss Grandma's teenage behavior with Julia Wilkes. I knock on Gram's door, and when she doesn't answer, I tiptoe inside. Just in case she's napping.

She isn't. She's sitting in her flowered chair

looking every bit as angry as my mom. When she sees me, she looks up. "He's late again," she snaps, shaking her head from side to side.

I say hello and kiss her powdery cheek, then plop down on the ottoman beside her. There's a crystal bowl full of chocolate-covered cherries on the windowsill, so I cram a big one in my mouth before asking, "Who?"

"That Fritz."

That Fritz. That Fritz is really starting to bug me.

"He's spending more and more time with Mrs. Knowles in room 136." Grandma leans closer and whispers, **"She bribes him with Liver Snaps."**

Ugh. I'll never understand boys. Or old men.

"Grandma, we need to talk about Fritz. They want to separate the two of you. Mom's meeting with the administrator right now arranging for you to move to the seventh floor."

Grandma's mouth drops open a little and her blue eyes glisten. "But Fritz isn't allowed on the seventh floor. I'd never get to see him."

Which confirms what I already knew. That Fritz is trouble. "Grandma, he's not good for you. Not only does he get you into trouble, but he takes off and lets you take the blame. And now he's cheating on you with Mrs. Knowles!"

"Cheating on me? I wouldn't call it cheating . . ."

Gram is too sweet and innocent for her own good. "Believe me, Gram, if he's so much as *looking* at another woman's Liver—"

"Shh! He's coming!" Grandma sits up taller and smoothes her gray curls. A pretty smile spreads across her face and I realize she's actually blushing. Two seconds later, the old collie who sleeps under the nurses' station walks in with a rubber toy in his mouth. He pads across the floor and sits in front of Gram, his feathery tail sweeping across the floor in pleasure. "Isn't Fritz magnificent?" she asks me.

"That's a dog, Grandma. It's Frisbee."

She snorts. "Ridiculous name for a dog." She scratches him behind the ear. "He prefers to be called Fritz."

Fritz's tail wags faster and he bites down on the toy in his mouth, which lets out a high-pitched squawk. Then he drops it at Gram's feet and I realize it's a rubber cigar.

I also realize **my grandma's special friend is no aging bad boy with a tobacco habit.** He's a beautiful old dog who obviously makes her very happy. She should be allowed to spend every moment with him.

But she can't do that from the seventh floor.

I grab Fritz's collar and coax him toward the hall.

"Where are you going with him?" Grandma calls out. "He's only just arrived . . ."

"We'll be right back, Grandma. There are a couple of people Fritz needs to meet."

If Your Father Loves You Enough to Paint You a Thundering Stallion, It's Your Duty to Never Look Away

Saturday morning is moving day. Not only do I have to lug suitcases and plants down to the car, I have to carry them down eight flights of stairs because the elevator is broken again. The moving men are grumbling and groaning, and one of them keeps swearing this is his last move. He's going to win the lottery and retire to an island in the Caribbean where someone can wait on him for a change. I stay away from him, since I'm pretty much all islanded out for the year.

Devon's family has moved out of the house. They haven't left town yet. I overheard my mom say they're staying with Devon's grandparents a few days before heading off to Boston for Mr. Sweeney's treatment. Of course, I haven't told anyone a thing. As far as the kids at Allencroft Middle School know, Devon Sweeney is here to stay.

Another person who's staying put is Grandma. Once the

people at Shady Gardens found out Gram's special friend is a collie, even Helga decided she's best off in her little bird-watching room with Fritz and his squeaky cigar.

I head back into my room to make sure I haven't forgotten anything. It's a good thing I did, too, because one of my favorite stuffed animals—Effie the elephant—is lying on the floor of my closet. She must have fallen out of a box. I lean over to scoop her up and catch sight of Horse on my wall.

I'll never get over how perfectly Dad painted Horse's head. The ears look all velvety like a real horse's ears, both of them pricked forward—like he's listening to the sounds in my bedroom. There's a white blaze zigzagging down the horse's face, and you can actually see every individual hair. It must have taken months for Dad to finish this.

Knowing that some other kid—or adult—will move into my room and probably paint right over Horse makes my stomach flip over. A painting like this deserves special protection. It needs a rule. Preferably an unwritten one.

It'll be **Unwritten Rule #19** and it will go something like this. **If your father loves you enough to paint** a thundering-hooved, flaring-nostriled, galloping stallion on your wall where you can see it each and every night when you go to sleep—and you don't have him around to paint you another—you should never, ever move away and leave it behind.

"Zoë," calls Mom. "It's time to get going."

It'll be the first unwritten rule I break the minute after I make it.

I stare at it real hard so I can remember every single detail. Mom walks into my room. "There you are. The new tenants are moving in here this afternoon, so we have to skedaddle, sweetheart. We'll stay at the hotel tonight—did you pack your bathing suit?"

I nod.

"Good. We'll swim, then go back to the room and order pizza; we'll even watch one of those overpriced movies in the hotel room. Then, tomorrow morning, the lawyer will give us our keys and the house will finally be ours. We'll move in." She comes closer and puts her arm around me. "Sound good?"

It sounds terrible. All of it. But she's so excited, I don't say so. "Mom?"

"Mm?"

"Is it possible to get the chicken pox twice? Because my head feels all swimmy again."

"No, babe. It's not possible."

Tears fill my eyes and I try to blink them back so she doesn't see.

"So, all set?" she asks.

I look at my horse again. "Can I take one last picture of it? I like the way it looks without all my furniture around it."

She smiles, then pulls her camera from her purse and hands it to me. I back up all the way until the far wall, aim, and snap. I'll never see Horse again in person.

As we head into the hall, we hear a scritch-scratching sound coming from the bathroom. "Wait, what's that?" I ask.

"Probably a whole family of cockroaches waiting to move in. Let's get going before they get our new address and follow us."

"But maybe it's . . ."

She shakes her head. "Not possible, sweetheart. He'd never have survived this long living in the walls of this old building. The mold alone would have killed him." Then she sees my horrified face and smiles. "Oh, I'm sorry. Boris is probably alive and living in the Dumpster out back."

I had to come clean with Mom about the whole guinea-pig swap when, a few days ago, I saw her heading into our bathroom with a can of bug spray. The last thing I want is for Boris to find his way home, starved and exhausted, only to have him perish by pesticides.

There goes the scratching again.

This time it sounds like it's coming from the bathroom cupboard. I rush into the tiny room, dive down onto my knees, and yank open the cup- board door. **Two beady eyes and a quivering nose are pointed up at me.**

Boris!

The next morning, me, my mom, and purring Boris pull up in front of the new house. It's been blizzarding all night, so the house is all covered in a big puffy blanket of snow and looks kind of cottagey and delicious. Like a gingerbread house covered in frosting. I can see that it would look kind of nice if smoke were com- ing out of the fireplace.

Dad would have loved this place.

Mom turns off the engine and hands me an envelope.

"What's this?" I ask.

"You'll see."

I rip it open and pull out two keys. One is a boring old silver one and the other is purple and covered in mod daisies. I look at my mother.

"Don't even think about taking the silver one," she says with a wink. "Because that one's mine."

I have to admit, my key is the coolest key I've ever had in my life.

"Go on," she says, nodding toward the house. "Go open your new front door."

I scoop up Boris's box and wade through the snowdrifts to the front door. Unlike our front door locks at the apartment, this lock turns easily and the door swings open. Inside, boxes are stacked against the walls and furniture sits facing in wrong directions in the middle of each room. I kick off my snowy boots and wander from room to room, showing Boris my new house. There are so many things I hadn't noticed the first time. Like the secret cupboard under the stairs. And the bookshelves in the den. And the way the stairs creak when you step on the middle of them—but not if you creep along the edge.

The upstairs hallway is dark, except for at the very end, where light is pouring out of my bedroom door. I slip and slide along the wooden floors in my socks, anxious to show

Boris my new room. In the doorway, I stop breathing so fast I make a sharp squeak.

There on my navy wall, staring down at me like he's waiting to see how I'll react, is Horse.

I start to laugh and cry all at once as I step closer. It's hard to see through my tears, but there's no question it's real actual Horse. I set Boris's box on the floor, rest my head against Horse's chest, and drink in the smell of him. I run my hands against the bumpity texture that is his legs, his strong shoulders. With my eyes closed, I move my hand up until I feel the smooth, ripply muscles of his neck.

I don't know how, I don't know who, I don't even know when, but somebody, somehow, cut away the wall in my old bedroom and hung it up here. And whoever did this for me didn't just give me a painting of a horse.

They gave me my dad back.

Suddenly Mom's arms wrap around me from behind and she rests her head against Horse, too.

"Thank you," I whisper.

She kisses the top of my head. "Your dad will always be with you, sweetheart. No matter where you go."

Don't Judge a Book by Its Hot-Pink Cover

Monday morning is my first day back at school after moving to the new house. We're celebrating Devon's Icktopian leadership by having juice boxes and pizza crusts at our desks. Mrs. Patinkin accidentally ordered less than half the number of pizzas that would normally feed a bunch of creatures like us. So we're all nibbling on crusts and dying for someone else to put theirs down so we can snatch it. At least Mrs. Patinkin said that if we're extra good about not stuffing pizza crusts into the heating vent, she'll bring out the special island-shaped cake she bought us.

We're also celebrating Boris and Doris's blind date, which began with her biting him in the shoulder and has moved on to the two of them disappearing behind the haystack to snuggle and poop. Everyone is congratulating Devon and asking her if her plans for Icktopia will ever appear in print.

Devon still hasn't told anyone about moving. But when Alice asked if island leadership was for life, Devon tilted her chin in the air and said, "Whether I rule for ten minutes or ten years isn't important. My friends believing in me is all that really matters."

Susannah rushes in, late. Today was the big day. The day she was supposed to get cast in her major motion picture. She hangs up her cape and slides into the seat beside me, pushing her sunglasses farther up her nose. Then she disappears behind a wall of Queen-of-the-Perfects hair.

Laurel and I push back the hair and peer at her. "So? Can we start shopping for a real loft now?" I ask.

"Hardly."

"You didn't get the part?" asks Laurel.

"Oh, I got the part all right. I play the 'before' role. Before the face cleanser. I saw the script. You know what my part is called?"

I shake my head.

"Pimple Girl!" She pulls her hair curtain shut and disappears.

Just as I'm thinking I could probably do a better job than her crummy agent—and for much less money—Riley grabs a chair and swings it over to my desk, then plops himself on top of it. He reaches up to brush pizza crumbs off my shoulder. "You did good yesterday, Monday."

Normally, I'd thump any kid who calls me Monday, but this is Riley and I can smell his shampoo. "Whatever. I just said what I felt."

He smiles with his eyes. But sad. "I've missed you."

"Me, too."

"Maybe you could come over after school today. Meet my new pets."

I grunt. "More hairy fish?"

"No. Two golden retrievers."

My eyebrows shoot up to the ceiling. "You mean, that really was dog hair?"

He nods, laughing. "What else could it have been?"

"I thought, since you kept going places with Devon, that it was . . ."

"You thought Devon was shedding on me?"

"Kinda."

Riley leans in to me with his very unhairy shoulder. "Zoë, my mom is friends with Devon's mom. I know all about . . . everything. Her family had to give away their dogs. We adopted them. I went to her house once to meet them. She came to my house one lunch to say good-bye to them. That's it."

My insides feel all chocolaty delicious. Devon didn't take Riley away from me! I blush and bump against his shoulder. "Golden retriever fur, huh?" I laugh. "That must be what I found in my new bedroom. The house we just moved into used to be Devon's."

Riley grins. "Seriously? Maybe I can bring the dogs over to visit after school. To see their old place?"

"That could be arranged," I say.

"You gave her a pretty awesome gift the other day," he says quietly.

I just shrug. Maybe I did, maybe I didn't. But one thing I know for sure, **Devon needs every bit of awesomeness she can dig up right about now.**

He gets up and bops me on the chin as he turns to go. Which is a little piece of awesomeness I very much adore.

"Psst, Zoë," says Sylvia from two seats behind me. She's holding her pizza crust, which looks like she's been pecking away at it without much luck. "I have a question for you."

"What's up?"

"I, um, I was wondering if you have any room on your

client roster. For a new client." She blushes. "Or maybe more of an apologetic old one."

I think about this for a second. What Sylvia doesn't know is that Devon is about to disappear from all of our lives. And that, like it or not, I'll be forced to take on her entire client list and add it to mine. **What else is a Lama to do? Leave gaggles of innocent friends to fend for themselves? It's a very complicated world out there.**

She needs me now more than ever. Not only to undo Devon's canine damage, but to help her with that nasty rash that seems to be developing on her chin. But somehow, I like that this is all her own doing. She's coming back to me because she wants to; she has no clue whatsoever, that as of tomorrow, she'll have no other options.

"Are you unhappy with your current representation?" I ask.

She tugs on her new necklace, which looks an awful lot like a dog's choke chain, and shrugs. "Kinda."

I try not to jumbo-smile while I reach for my client book and pretend to scan through an enormous list that isn't nearly as enormous as it used to be. "Let's see now. I think I might be able to squeeze you in. You're absolutely sure about this?"

Sylvia nods and I jump up and shake her hand so hard, I'm afraid I might injure her delicate wing bones. "Welcome to Zoë Lama and Associates, Sylvia."

"Um, Zoë?"

"Yeah?"

"If it's all right with you, I prefer plain old Zoë Lama. I think I like it that way the best."

I think about this for a moment. "You know what? Maybe I do, too."

She pulls a carton of milk from her desk. Not her usual brand either. In fact, if I'm not mistaken, it looks very much like the milk Brandon drinks. She sees me staring and giggles. "Brandon brought it for me. In case I got thirsty during the Icktopia party."

I glance over at Brandon, who's waggling his worn-down LameWizard fingers at her from the corner of the room. Sylvia waves back.

Just then, Mrs. Patinkin walks in the door with an island-shaped cake. The outside edges are blue frosting and plastic palm trees decorate the center. ICKTOPIA is written across the island in loopy pink icing. Smartin shouts,

"Cool! when he sees the plastic shark lurking in the north-ern waters.

She sets the cake down on her desk and hands a knife to Devon. "And now, if our new leader will do us the honor of slicing the Icktopian cake . . ."

Devon takes the knife and starts to slice off a surfer in a gnarly wave, but she stops and looks around, her face going red. "I can't do this, Mrs. Patinkin. I think . . . I think I have to resign as leader."

"If it's because of our forbidden love," says Smartin, "don't worry. The Icktopian people are pretty cool about that sort of thing."

She almost laughs. "No. It's because I'm moving. To-morrow. To Boston, and I'm not coming back. I was afraid to say anything because I wanted to win this election so very, very bad, but now I can see I ruined it. You've elected me and now you're going to have no leader. The Icktopian people will be without the guidance they so richly deserve—"

"Devon," Mrs. Patinkin said, "while we'll all be very sorry to see you go, our government unit is now finished. As of tomorrow, we'll begin to study weather patterns in the North and South poles. I'm afraid the Icktopian people will be no more."

Up goes Alice Marriott's hand. "Devon? Why do you have to move?"

For a second, Devon's face looks strained. Like she's been hit in the chest and is trying to pretend it didn't take her breath away. Then it passes. "My father wants us to be close to Harvard," she says. "It's where he's always wanted me and my sister to go to college. My father always says, 'You can never plan too early.'"

It might be true. Devon didn't actually say it was *the* reason. It's very possible that being close to Harvard is something he's always dreamed of. But what she's not saying is that her father is having a lung transplant. And that he needs to get the very best medical care if he's going to survive.

I hope that he does.

Just before 3:15 all the kids line up to get Devon to autograph her book. Maisie even said she was going to put hers away and sell it on eBay once Devon gets her own TV show. It would have to be a show on how to housebreak a Lhasa apso, but I don't say a word. I'm last in line. When I slap my copy of "Devon Says" on her desk, she looks extra happy. "Seriously? I always thought you hated my written rules."

"Nah. You're a published author, Devon. A girl's got to respect that."

"Well, thanks."

"No problem."

After she writes "Devon," she starts to draw a big swirl-ing *s* but I stop her. "Can you do me a favor? Can you sign it 'Devon Lama'?"

She smiles so wide, she squeaks.

Watching her sign "Devon Lama" just about knocks me sideways. But I can handle being knocked sideways now and then. My dad will always be with me, no matter what. I know that now. Devon will know it, too, someday. But for now, she really does need every speck of happiness she can get.